Tollie and Patch were getting up. They had been flattened, but they hadn't lost hold of their pistols.

Patch got to his knees and fired, shooting off the heel of Strate's left boot.

Strate lost his balance and fell to the floor, firing as he fell.

Tollie was hit and pitched backward into the wall. His pistol fired into the ceiling.

Patch didn't waste a shot. He was standing now, and he stepped quickly over to Strate and kicked him in the head.

Strate's teeth slapped together and his mind went black. He didn't even hear his head hit the wooden floor.

GALVESTON GUNMAN

Bill Crider

BALLANTINE BOOKS • NEW YORK

Library of Congress Catalog Card Number: 88-37362

ISBN 0-345-36531-3

This edition published by arrangement with M. Evans & Co.

Manufactured in the United States of America

First Ballantine Books Edition: March 1990

For Francelle and Ellen:
It's their turn

Chapter One

Lee Strate went to Houston for the same reason that he'd come to Texas in the first place, and for the same reason that he'd done nearly everything else since leaving Kansas.

Money.

Money wasn't all of it, not at first. At first there had been the desire to see if there was more to the world than flatland farming, than looking out and seeing miles and miles of unbroken prairie, nothing to break the sight at all unless you looked in the direction of a house, nothing until you came to the horizon that always looked the same.

One man in Strate's hometown had planted a tree. Everyone had thought he was crazy, or if not crazy, at least a bit strange. Everyone, that is, except for Strate. There were times when he understood exactly why that man had planted the tree, and there were times when he just wanted to stand and look at it, but he seldom did. Too much of that and people would have thought he was crazy, too.

No one thought he was crazy, but they did think him a little strange, and three years previously, when he was twenty-five years old, he told his father that he was leaving.

His father didn't understand. Why would anyone want to leave Kansas? Sure, there had been some rough times there for a while, but Lee was too young to have suffered much from the war and its attendant troubles. Bloody Kansas was

1

just a memory now, the farm was making money, and if the work was hard, the rewards were worth it. There were plenty of young women in town who would have been proud to be the wife of one of the Strate boys, and if Lee could just settle down. . . .

That was just it. Lee couldn't settle down. There was too much he wanted to do and see.

"What?" his father demanded. His father was a tall, gaunt man with a passing resemblance to the late President Lincoln, and his demands were not to be taken lightly.

So Lee tried to explain. He couldn't really say, however, because he hadn't done and seen. One thing he knew, though: There had to be more to life than sowing and planting and harvesting. Lee's hand went to the ridge on his neck, rubbed there by the plow lines from all the time he'd spent following after the mules, felt it with a hand rubbed smooth and hard by the plow handle. He was tall and gaunt, like his father, but some freak of inheritance had given him a shock of stiff red hair. No one knew where it had come from—some forgotten ancestor, perhaps. It was just one more thing that made him different.

"I just want to go," he said. "See what's out there." He gestured vaguely in the direction he thought he might go, which happened to be west.

"Nothin' out there you can't find here," his father told him, but Lee knew that wasn't true. There was more. There had to be.

At that, Lee's thoughts were not that much different from those of a lot of young men in the late 1870s, young men in a growing country that seemed to hold out to them some kind of vague promise, a promise of something new, something exciting, something that wasn't tied to plow lines or mules. What it was they didn't exactly know, but a great many of them went looking for it.

It wasn't a woman. Lee's father was right about that. There were plenty of women right there at home, and one or two of them were going to be mighty sorry to see Lee go.

It wasn't even that he wanted to get away from his family. He loved his father and his three older brothers, would no doubt have loved his mother if he had ever known her. She had died when he was only two.

And it wasn't the work, either. It was hard, bone-wearying work, but Lee didn't mind that. There were even times when he enjoyed it. It had made him strong, flattened his belly, and given him powerful arms and hands, the kind of arms and hands that made men think twice before arguing with him for very long.

No, it was none of those things. It was simply a vague, undefined longing that had to be satisfied.

His father finally saw there was no stopping him. "How do you plan to make a living?" he said. "I can give you a little money—God knows you've earned it—but it won't last forever."

Lee hadn't really thought about that, but it didn't worry him. "I'll find something," he said. "There's always something for a man who's not afraid of a little work."

"I hope you'll wait till after the spring plowing, then," his father said in a resigned voice. "I'll be needing your help at least till then. After that maybe I can hire some of the work done."

"I'll wait," Lee said, but he didn't see how he could.

He did, though.

When the time finally came to leave, he shook hands with his brothers and his father, wished them well, and walked away. Two of the brothers were married already, and the third had spoken for the Wilkes girl. They looked wistfully at his back as he strolled down the dirt road toward town. They would miss him, but that wasn't the reason for the look in their eyes. Lee would have known that look if he had turned around to see it. It had been in his own eyes when he heard train whistles at night, or when he had seen the engines steaming out of the depot. He would have understood, all right, but he didn't look back. He was too busy looking ahead.

His plan was to get as far as he could the first day. He didn't have a horse, and he didn't want to spend his money for a train ticket, but he didn't mind walking. Besides, he had an idea that he hadn't told his father about, or his brothers. He thought that it just might be possible to steal a ride on the train, on an empty car or even on the rods beneath the car. It was dangerous, but that didn't bother him.

The plan also included a horse, but that was for later, when he had more money. For now he would have to travel the best way he could.

There was one other thing in the plan—a gun. Hardly anyone in the little farming community carried one these days. It didn't seem necessary. No one had ever tried to rob the bank, mainly because there wasn't enough money in it to bother with, and snakes and other varmints were a rarity. But he had heard that a man needed a gun in the West, for personal protection and sometimes even as a way to earn money.

Yes, he would have to have a gun. With a gun and a horse there would be no stopping him. He would see and do all the things he wanted to see and do, whatever those were, and the promise would be fulfilled.

It had all seemed just that easy three years before, but Lee Strate had learned a lot in those three years.

He had seen plenty, all right, cow towns and mining towns, big cities, trees aplenty, even the ocean, but it hadn't meant all he thought it would.

He had ridden the rods and he had ridden in plush cars with red stuffed cushions on the seats. He had his own horse now. But he still wasn't sure that he had what he wanted.

He had the gun, too, a single-action Colt .45, the one some people called the Peacemaker, though as far as he knew, it wasn't used primarily for making peace. He had turned out to be good with the gun—not fast, but careful, deliberate, accurate. He had used it for a job or two, but he wasn't proud of that.

And he had the money. Or he *had* had it. Or had had it and now he didn't. That was why he went to Houston.

The money was five thousand dollars, not a bad sum at all, and every time he thought about it, Lee Strate cursed himself for losing it, although *losing* wasn't exactly the right word.

It had been stolen from him, and he had let it go like

some dumb kid, some greenhorn, someone who hadn't been off the farm for more than three days instead of three years.

It had happened right after he left a little East Texas town called Nacogdoches. He had been on his way to Colorado, or at least that's what he had told the few people he trusted. When you're carrying five thousand dollars that some people might think they had more of a right to than you, you didn't always tell the truth about your destination to anyone.

As it was, he'd been traveling more in the direction of San Antonio than Denver, riding the palomino gelding he'd bought more than a year before. He was still about a day's ride from San Antonio when he made camp one night in a little grove of oak trees.

He built a fire and boiled some coffee. He had a little jerked beef that he was going to eat for his supper, and he was looking forward to getting into town and eating some real food in the next day or so. He wasn't much of a trail cook, and maybe it was thinking about the food that he was going to have that made him careless. When he thought about it afterward, he was sure that was it.

He didn't even hear the man come up. It was like one minute he wasn't there and the next he was, standing right there at the edge of the trees, just outside the firelight, holding his horse's reins in his hand.

He was a small, scruffy-looking man, no more than five feet tall. He hadn't shaved in quite a while, but then, neither had Strate. His clothes looked trail-worn and dusty, as best Strate could tell in the faint light from the fire. He wore a beat-up hat, and when he talked, he seemed to have a mouthful of mush.

"Coffee smells mighty good," he said.

Strate listened, but he heard nothing back in the trees, no rustle of leaves, no whiffle of a horse's breath, no rattle of a bridle.

The little man stood right where he was, not intruding into the firelight any farther, not saying anything else. He had a hangdog look about him that said he wasn't about to come any closer if he wasn't invited.

It wasn't a dark night, but it was darker in the grove.

Strate strained his eyes into the blackness behind the little man to see if there were any shadows moving back in there, shadows that might be something else.

He didn't see anything.

"Come on up to the fire," he said. "Have a cup." What the hell, a man so small was bound to be harmless.

"Don't mind if I do," the man said, stepping fully into the circle of the firelight.

He made a great deal of noise, scuffing his boots in the leaves and sticks, jangling his bridle, and keeping up a train of patter. "Yessir, it's been quite a spell since I had me any real good coffee. Been quite a spell since I had me anything at all worth the talkin' about. I 'spect I'm really gonna enjoy this."

He was to the fire by then, reaching for the rag that Strate used to wrap the handle of the coffeepot when he poured. As the man bent down, Strate heard the other noise, but by then it was too late.

The others had come up behind him, and they had gotten close when their partner had come scuffing and talking up to the fire, the sound of his coming drowning out their own.

Strate tried to stand and turn, but he got only halfway up and around before something hit him in the side of the head. It felt like a tree, but it was only a solid oak limb. He hit the ground and slid on his side, away from the fire.

He shook his head and tried to see who had hit him. There were two men, one of them wearing a black patch over his left eye. Strate got the impression of a cruel smile and a hooked nose.

The other man was black, wearing a dirty flannel shirt and a hat that looked as if a horse had stepped on it.

That was about all the look Strate got, because the man with the patch walked over and kicked him under the chin. Strate's teeth clapped together, and he went over and out.

He didn't know how long he was unconscious, but it couldn't have been long. When he came to, he heard the men talking.

"God a'mighty, Patch, I never seen so much money. Where you reckon he got it?" That was Mush-mouth.

"I don't know," someone answered in a voice as cold and hard as rocks in a mountain river. Patch, no doubt. "You can bet he didn't get it honest, so he won't mind if we take it."

There was a deep, rich laugh. The black man. "Like hell he won't. *Anybody* minds if you take his money. Don't matter how he got it or how much it is."

Patch laughed, too, but it didn't sound like laughter. It sounded like river rocks grinding together. "I should've said he won't mind, as long as he don't know about it."

"Money like that, we won't have to go to Houston." Mush-mouth said. "Money like that, we can go just about anywhere we want to go. Go to Mexico if we got a mind to. Never come back." There was something wistful in his tone.

"We can't do that," Patch said. He was clearly the leader. "The Colonel sent for us to come to Houston, and that's where we're goin'."

"We're gonna keep the money, though?" Mush-mouth.

Patch laughed again. "Like I said, he won't mind. Kill him, Tollie."

Strate didn't know which of them was Tollie, but he didn't have in mind to be killed by anybody—not then, not ever. Since there was no need to lie quiet any longer, he went for his gun.

The black man had turned toward Strate, his own gun out, when Strate fired. The slug hit the black man in the upper arm, spinning him around and into Patch.

The black man yelled, and Strate got up running. He didn't fancy his chances against the three of them, or even two, if the black man was hurt too bad to fight. He hated the very thought of leaving behind his five thousand dollars, but there was no way he could spend it if he was dead.

There were enough trees to hide in, he hoped, and maybe he could circle around and get to his horse, which was hobbled nearby. It wasn't much of a plan, but it was the only one he had.

The men in the clearing untangled themselves and began firing at Strate. He could hear the bullets ripping through the leaves around him and thudding into the trunks of trees.

Then one slapped into his pant leg and gouged a good-sized hunk of flesh from his left calf.

He went down, doing a clumsy somersault, the first he'd done since he was around five years old. By the time he could sit up again, his calf was burning as if someone had stuck a chunk of coal to it. He had to bite his lip to keep from crying out.

He had landed right by a fallen tree, not a very big one, but one that had somehow rotted from the inside and fallen over. He squirmed down to the top branches and hid himself in them as best he could, waiting for the three men to come after him.

They never came.

He heard them beating around the trees for a few minutes, now and then firing off a shot, but after that things got quiet. Then he heard their horses moving off. They wanted him dead, but they didn't *need* him dead. After all, they had the money.

For a while he just lay there, feeling the burning in his calf, the scratching of the bare tree branches, the wetness of his blood on his pants. He felt like a fool, falling for a stupid trick like that one. Serve him right if he lay there and let himself bleed to death.

If he did that, though, he'd never get the money back.

He sat up and tore off his pant leg below the knee. He made a crude tourniquet and started back to the fire. If they hadn't taken his clean shirt, he could make a bandage, and he had a little whiskey in a bottle in his saddlebags. He could use the whiskey to clean the wound.

They hadn't taken his clean shirt, but they had taken the whiskey.

"Bastards," Strate said, but there was no heat in it. He blamed himself, thought he had gotten exactly what he deserved. He'd been so sure he was in no danger, that he could take care of himself. One thing he thought he'd learned in his three years of traveling was that there were very few people you could trust, and you could never trust anyone you'd just met. Yet he'd let Mush-mouth walk right into his camp.

He'd heard that you could cleanse a wound with fire, and he still had the fire. He could take the coal and see if it would burn him any worse than he already was burning, then bandage the leg. He hoped he didn't pass out. He didn't think he would, but he'd never tried anything like that before. But then he'd never been shot before, either.

He looked at the wound, hoping that it wouldn't be bad enough to require the cleaning. It looked bad enough. He didn't want his leg to rot off. He'd heard that could happen if you let wounds go untended.

He took a stick from the fire. The end was black and the tip was glowing red.

Might as well get it over with, he thought.

Chapter Two

When he woke up, it was as if his whole body had caught fire from the place on his calf. The sun was shining down through the trees, and at first he thought that the sun was burning him. Then he decided that he had a fever.

The only good thing he could think of was that at least he hadn't passed out when he cauterized the wound. He had put a stick in his mouth and bitten down hard—almost snapping the stick, in fact—but he hadn't passed out.

Well, not right then. He had managed to get the bandage on before he fell over on his side and lost consciousness.

And now he was cold. At first he had been hot, but now he was cold. He needed a blanket to pull over him, but he knew he didn't have one. He wasn't sure he would have been able to reach it, anyway.

He thought that he'd better sleep for a while.

He woke up again, feeling the grit under his cheek. Something was crawling across the back of his hand, and he shook it off.

The sun was still shining on him, and he wasn't cold anymore. He was hot again.

Something moved nearby, and he turned his head.

There was a black man squatting a few feet away. Not Tollie. This man was not as big as Tollie, and he looked older, though not by much.

"Who . . . who are you?" Strate said.

"I 'swan, whitefolks, I thought you be dead sho' 'nuff."

Strate, sure that he must be dreaming, went back to sleep.

It was dark the next time he woke, and he could smell a fire. His head was clear enough for him to realize that it couldn't be the fire he had lit the previous night. He tried to turn over and found that he had been covered with a ragged blanket.

"You lie still, now, whitefolks. You let ole Jack take care of you and you be jus' fine."

Strate could see the man now, sitting by the fire.

"I got us some soup here," the man said. "I be feedin' it to you by 'n' by."

Strate got himself up on his elbow. "You really talk like that?"

The man's eyes looked red in the firelight. "Not always."

"Good," Strate said. "Your name really Jack?"

"That is correct. Jack Farmer. Just rest and don't ask so many questions. The soup should be ready soon."

Strate lay back. He could smell the soup now, along with the fire. He could smell the blanket, too, but it had a clean, fresh smell in spite of being considerably the worse for wear.

After ten or fifteen minutes Jack helped him sit up. Jack had spooned some of the soup into a tin cup, and he began feeding it to Strate a little at a time. It was very hot, so hot that Strate couldn't make out the flavor. It burned his tongue and the roof of his mouth.

When he complained, Jack said, "Never mind that. Just eat it. You'll feel better if you do."

Strate had no idea why he should believe this black man, but he did. He sipped the soup, trying to swallow it immediately so as not to hold it in his mouth any longer than was absolutely necessary.

He took all that was in the cup.

"That's very good," Jack said.

"What was in that stuff?" Strate asked.

"You don't need to know that. Good things. Go back to

sleep." Jack was spooning more soup into the cup, obviously getting ready to eat some himself.

Strate thought that was fine advice.

Jack checked the wound the next day. "You did a good job," he said. "Too bad you didn't have any hog fat to put on it. Hog fat's good for things like that. But you'll be all right. There's no infection. The shock and loss of blood just put you a little under the weather for a while."

Strate was feeling much better, almost his normal self again, though he had tried to stand up and found his leg still a little weak. "I'm glad you stopped by. I'm not sure I could have made it through without that soup."

"You would have made it, but you might have been somewhat less comfortable. I'm glad I was able to help."

Strate looked all around the clearing. His saddle was still there, and his saddlebags. He didn't see his horse, however.

"You didn't see a palomino around here, did you?" he asked.

"No," Jack said. "No horse at all. Just old William there." He glanced to his right to indicate the flop-eared mule tied to a tree nearby.

Strate cursed. That they had taken his money was bad enough, but they had even taken his horse.

"You've obviously had some sort of difficulty here," Jack said. He made it a simple statement. He wasn't asking anything.

Strate decided to tell him, anyway. "Three men came into my camp the other night, before you found me. They robbed me, took my horse. Shot me, too."

"I knew about the shooting," Jack said.

"Why did you stop?" Strate said. "Most people would have just gone on by."

"Someone did me a good turn once. He told me that the only way I could return the favor was by doing good for others. I've tried to do that."

"He must have been an unusual person," Strate said.

Jack nodded. "He was."

Strate lapsed into silence, wondering what to do next. He

had no money, and he had no horse. He certainly didn't feel a lot like walking.

Then he remembered what he had heard one of the men say: "The Colonel sent for us to come to Houston, and that's where we're goin'."

"Which way were you headed when you stopped here?" he asked Jack.

"No place in particular," Jack said. "I had a letter from a man I know in San Antonio. He said there might be a job there for me."

Strate suddenly decided that he could trust Jack. He didn't know why he thought so. After all, he had just made the mistake of trusting another stranger and inviting him to share his fire. He thought about it for a minute. What the hell, if you couldn't trust a man who'd given you a blanket and fed you soup, who could you trust?"

"I want to go to Houston," he told Jack.

"Why would you want to do that?" Jack asked.

"For five thousand dollars. That's what those men took from me."

Jack looked at him skeptically. He was younger than Strate had first thought, probably no older than Tollie after all, but his tightly curled hair was already quite white at the temples and on the sides. His face, however, was smooth and unlined.

"Where'd a man like you get that much money?" Jack asked.

Strate looked him in the eyes and didn't say a word.

"I'm sorry," Jack said. "I shouldn't have asked that."

"It's all right," Strate said. "But I'm not going to tell you."

"I don't really want to know," Jack said.

"Good. Now the problem is, I don't have any way to get to Houston, and you've got that mule."

Jack shook his head. "William's not for sale."

"I didn't want to buy him."

"He's not for rent, either. William's *my* mule."

"I can't afford to rent him. Those men took all my money." Strate felt in the pocket of his pants. He hadn't told the whole truth. He had a silver dollar. He pulled it out and held it up. "Almost all my money."

"What are you trying to say, then?"

"I want you to take me to Houston. Let me ride that mule."

They both looked over at William, whose ears perked up as if he knew what was being discussed.

"You want me to walk, and you get to ride?"

"I think you're in a little better shape for walking than I am," Strate said. "But I don't care if you ride. As long as I can ride with you."

"And for this you'll pay me a dollar? No thank you, sir. Slavery times are over."

"Who said anything about a dollar?" Strate was getting upset, and he could feel his body getting hot under his shirt. "I'll pay you from the five thousand dollars when I get it back."

"Ah," Jack said. "I see it now. And how were you planning to get it back?"

Strate really hadn't thought that far ahead. He supposed that he would locate the Colonel, force him to divulge the location of Patch and the others, and beat them to a pulp. Then he would get his money.

He told Jack what he thought.

"That sounds like a highly speculative venture," Jack said.

Strate admitted that it did. "But so's that job that you might or might not get in San Antonio."

"True, but the job, if I did get it, would not be dangerous."

"If you get me to Houston and help me find those men, I'll give you a thousand dollars," Strate said.

"I think business partners should know one another's names," Jack said. "You haven't told me yours."

"Strate, Lee Strate."

"All right, Lee, I'll help you get to Houston. Let me ask William if he would mind carrying double."

Strate sighed. He didn't like the idea of riding a mule, much less one that was carrying double, but he did want to get his money back, and the only way to do that was to go to Houston. He hoped that William was agreeable.

It turned out that he was.

It was early summer, the weather was warm, and William was not particularly inclined to a rapid pace. Strate was sure that he could have walked faster, if he could have walked.

"Have you ever been to Houston?" he asked Jack the next day, not long after they had started out.

"No, I never have," Jack said. "I've heard it's not the kind of place you go by choice."

"Are you sure that this is the right direction?" The trail that they were traveling was just that—a trail. Strate thought that the way to a city should have been more clearly defined.

"It's the way the men who attacked you went," Jack said. "We should come to a road sooner or later."

Strate was surprised. He hadn't even thought of tracking the three men. Growing up on the farm hadn't given him any opportunity for tracking, and his experiences since then had not been conducive to learning.

"Have you done much tracking?" he asked.

"Not enough to qualify as an expert. These men weren't trying to hide anything. Otherwise I wouldn't have been able to do much."

Riding double on the mule was not comfortable, at least for Strate. He had only a blanket to sit on, whereas Jack had a saddle, and William's back was bony. Strate had been forced to leave his own saddle behind. There was no way to carry it, and Jack had not thought that William would stand for two saddles. The blanket Strate sat on was the same one he had found himself covered with, but he was willing to bet that it would no longer smell clean.

Although their progress was slow and uncomfortable, the journey was not too bad. There were plenty of streams for water, the sun never got too hot, and Jack was an excellent cook. Strate shot a rabbit the first day, and Jack made a stew that was better than anything Strate had eaten in a long time.

As they ate, Strate told Jack a little about his past, though not about how he had obtained the five thousand dollars, and Jack opened up a bit as well.

He had been born into slavery in Missouri around 1848. "I'm not sure exactly when," he said. "It was just a small farm, and they didn't keep very good records."

He had come to the attention of his master pretty early in life because of his intelligence. There was nowhere that he could go to school, but his master arranged to tutor him in the evenings whenever he could. "I picked up reading and writing very well," Jack said, "but mathematics never appealed to me. That was a big disappointment."

He didn't say who was disappointed, but Strate assumed it was the master.

"I was still young when the war began," Jack said. "Our master knew what was coming, and he set us all free right before it started. The only slaves he had were my family. Everyone stayed right there on his farm, even me, right through the war."

The others had stayed even after the war, but Jack had taken to the road. There were not many opportunities for a free black man in the South, and for fifteen or so years Jack had taken this job and that, doing what he could to earn a small living.

"I wouldn't have traded my way of life for the farm, though," Jack said. "It was safe there, and probably not uncomfortable, but I was the one who got to see things and try something different."

Strate thought that they seemed to have similar outlooks, but he didn't say so. His family had never owned slaves, but he still didn't quite feel comfortable thinking that he and this black man had so much in common.

"Why did you talk the way you did when you first found me?" he asked Jack.

Jack laughed. "I've learned that sometimes a man has to hide what he really is in order to lead a long life. There are some white men, even wounded ones, who might not take kindly to the idea of a black man sitting in their camp unless they were sure the black man was utterly harmless. I try to give them someone they'll feel comfortable with."

"That must not feel very good most of the time," Strate said.

"It never lasts for very long," Jack said.

"You're not carrying a gun, either," Strate said.

"I've found that if you don't carry one, you don't usually need one," Jack said. "Besides, I don't have five thousand dollars to protect."

"Who's the man who did you the favor?" Strate asked. He knew that it wasn't a proper question. It was entirely too personal, but he was feeling comfortable. His leg had almost stopped hurting, the stew filling his stomach had been delicious, and the night was warm and pleasant.

Jack didn't answer at first. He gathered up the tin plates they had used and took them down to the little creek near the camp to wash them out.

When he came back, he sat down and looked at Strate. "It was my master," he said. "His name was Thomas Carpenter, and he was a good man as far as he understood goodness. He never beat me or a member of my family, as far as I know. He taught me to read and write, and he tried to teach me something about mathematics. Not many men at that time and place would have done the same. He freed us before he had to, and he paid us fairly when we stayed on at his place. When I left there, I asked him if there was anything I could do to repay him for teaching me. What he said was what I've already told you."

Strate had been to school and done a little reading himself. He had read, for one thing, the parable of the Good Samaritan, and he was glad that Jack Farmer had been the one to come along when he was lying in the grove after being beaten by robbers. Things were bad, sure enough, but they could have been a whole lot worse.

Chapter Three

The area where the city of Houston had been established was declared by an early Spanish explorer to be unfit for human habitation, a fact that was either unknown to, or ignored by, the region's early settlers. The frequent rains turned the soil to a sticky gumbo, the air was filled with hordes of bloodthirsty mosquitoes, and the oppressive heat and humidity held sway for most of the year. In the winter it was still humid, but it was sometimes quite cold, especially when one of the famous Texas blue northers came sweeping down from the Arctic.

It was not raining when William carried his double burden into town, but the sky was overcast and there was an occasional low rumble of thunder. The temperature was high, and Strate felt almost as if he had been wrapped in a hot, wet sheet, except that it might have been easier to breathe in the sheet.

It had rained recently, and William's feet made slurping, sucking noises as he made his way down the street. Several people looked up as the mule walked by, wondering at the strange sight. Strate's leg was much better, and he would have gotten down and walked if it had not been for the mud. He imagined that it would stick to his boots like a mustard plaster, and he noticed that none of the people watching him strayed far off the board sidewalks.

One man a block away was crossing the street, trying awkwardly to extract one foot at a time from the thick goo and find a solid spot to set his boot before removing the other foot. He was making slow progress.

A couple of wagons in the street moved almost as slowly, their wheels sinking deep into the mud. The spokes were caked with the stuff, and in some places it had begun to harden.

"I can see what you meant about coming here," Strate said.

"It's not just the weather that keeps people away," Jack said, slapping at a mosquito that had settled on his neck. Strate could hear them singing around his head, too.

"Now that we're here," Jack said, "what kind of plan do you have for finding those men you're looking for?"

"I've been thinking about that," Strate said. He looked at the buildings that lined Main Street, solid two-story structures, some with wrought-iron columns and railings. Down the way there were workmen swarming over a building that was going to have four or five stories when it was completed. "I don't think they'd be in this part of town."

What he suspected was that men like Patch and Tollie and the other one most likely would be located in one of the city's less savory areas, somewhere they could buy drinks and women with his money and not be asked too many questions. The thought of them spending his money made his stomach ache.

"Any particular part of town that you have in mind?" Jack asked.

"Just keep going. We'll come to it." Though Strate had never been in Houston before, he was confident that its main street, like those of other places he had visited, would eventually lead to some places that were less than respectable.

He was right. It was already a part of Houston's dream to have a deep-water port, though the one they had now was only deep enough to annoy a man who tried to walk across it with his shoes on. Still, there was the beginning of a shipping industry, and before long, Strate saw freight wagons practically bogged down in the muddy street.

The buildings here were warehouses and saloons, ramshackle frame structures with rough shingle roofs and warped siding. There were no women on the streets here, and the men in the wagons and on the boardwalks looked hard and tough.

"May as well stop here," Strate said, indicating a place with the name SALTY DOG painted on it in blue letters. The letters were not exactly straight, and in fact the sign looked as if it had been painted by someone who was doing the job after a few drinks that were no doubt served inside.

"Are you planning to go in there?" Jack asked.

That was indeed Strate's plan, and he said so.

"And ask if anybody knows those men?"

"Yes," Strate admitted.

"And you think somebody's going to tell you if they do?"

"Why not?" Strate said, but he already knew the answer. He had been on the receiving end of such questions himself, in different circumstances, and he knew that the questioner was not likely to be given a warm welcome.

"It's just that I hate to see you get killed before I get my money," Jack said. "I surely do wish I'd gone on to San Antonio like I started to."

"Don't worry about me," Strate said. "I can look out for myself."

Jack nodded. "That's why you were doing so well when I happened upon you."

Strate didn't like the way the conversation was going. "Do you have a better idea?"

"Unfortunately, no."

"Well, let's get on with it, then."

Jack twitched the reins and directed the mule to the hitch rail in front of the Salty Dog. The rail was no more than a cedar post, its ends nailed to two other posts set in the mud.

"I'll wait out here," Jack said.

It was still the middle of the morning, and the inside of the Salty Dog was quiet. The door stood open to the street, but the light was so dim inside that Strate couldn't see what, if anything, was in there. "Why don't you just come with me?" he said.

"I told you that I was an educated man," Jack said. "I learned enough to stay out of places like that when there might be trouble."

Strate saw his point. He had offered Jack the money to take him to Houston, not to do his work for him or take his risks. "All right," he said. "I'll be back in a few minutes."

"I'll be here," Jack said.

Strate pushed himself back, pulled his left leg up and over, and slid down off the mule. There was a slight twinge in his calf as he sank down into the mud.

The Salty Dog had a wooden porch with one wooden step up to it. There was hardened mud on the edges of the boards where the patrons had scraped their boots. Strate kicked at the mud and tried to scrape the soles of his own boots before he went in, but the mud still adhered to the edges of the soles and to the leather uppers.

Strate walked inside the door and stopped, allowing his eyes to become accustomed to the dim light. The place had only one window, and it was so coated with grime that even if the sun had been shining, it would not have been able to penetrate the room.

There was a makeshift bar to Strate's left, and the rest of the room was taken up by six or seven rickety wooden tables. The only people that Strate could see were the bartender and two men sitting at one of the tables.

He walked over to the bar. The bartender was a burly man wearing an apron that looked as if it had last been washed at about the time Strate had left Kansas. His arms were thick and hairy, and he was leaning on the bar, looking at nothing in particular with his beady little eyes. He didn't look Strate's way, and neither did the two men.

"How about a drink," Strate said. "Whiskey."

The bartender looked at him without interest, raised himself up, and reached under the bar. He came out with a glass that looked a lot like the window, and a bottle of brownish liquid.

He poured the whiskey in the glass. "Two bits," he said. His voice was oddly high for such a big man.

Strate laid his dollar on the bar and took a swallow. He managed not to gag, though the stuff he had drunk burned all the way down to his stomach. He blinked once or twice and said. "I'm looking for a fella."

"Yeah," the bartender said. He had laid down Strate's change, and now he was leaning on the bar again, looking at nothing.

"He wears a patch over his left eye and travels with a black man named Tollie and a little mush-mouthed man."

The bartender turned his head idly. "You makin' fun of the way a man talks?"

Strate tried another sip of his drink. It was just as bad as the first one. "No," he said when he could talk again. "I have some business with him, that's all."

"Never saw anybody like that," the bartender said. He turned away.

Strate finished the drink. Waste not, want not. He put down the glass and swept up his change. He couldn't afford to ask too many questions at this rate. He looked around the room again and walked out.

It had begun to rain, a slow, steady drizzle. Jack was still sitting on the mule.

Strate slopped through the mud and climbed on somewhat unsteadily.

"You find out anything?" Jack asked.

"Nope."

"You planning on going to every saloon in this town and asking your questions?"

"I don't know what else to do. Did you think of anything while you were sitting out here?"

"Nothing but how much I'd like to get out of the rain."

The water was beginning to soak into Strate's clothes. It wasn't really unpleasant, he thought. The heavy, gray sky gave the impression of winter, but the rain was soft and warm, almost soothing.

"Let's try another couple of places," he said.

Jack pulled on the reins and clucked to the mule, which turned his head and started back into the street.

They had gone only three steps when someone hissed behind them.

Strate looked back. One of the men who had been sitting in the Salty Dog was standing on the porch. "Pssst," he said. He was motioning to them with his right hand.

"Turn around," Strate said. "I think somebody wants to talk to us."

"Probably wants you to buy him a drink," Jack said, but he turned the mule around. William's hoofs made a schlucking sound as they pulled out of the mud.

When they were stopped by the hitch rail again, the man continued to motion to them but said nothing. He was not old—not more than thirty, Strate thought—but he was stooped, as if he had spent a long, hard life breaking rocks with a sledge. He hadn't shaved for a while, and he could have used a bath. His clothes were almost as dirty as the bartender's apron.

"What can we do for you?" Strate said.

The man put his finger to his lips, then motioned for Strate to step up on the porch.

Strate didn't want to get into the mud again, but he slipped off the mule and climbed the step.

The man grabbed his sleeve and pulled him aside from the open door. "You lookin' for Patch?" he said. His voice rasped as if he had a throat full of phlegm.

"That's right," Strate said. "You know him?"

"I might. You a friend of his?"

"Not exactly. I just want to talk to him."

"How much would it be worth to you?" The man pulled his dirty sleeve across his mouth.

Strate looked at the rain running off the porch roof and at Jack sitting on William's back. Jack's clothes were sticking to him by now, the rain soaking through the heavy cloth.

"Look," Strate said, his voice hard. "I don't have enough money to buy a room for the night and a good meal. And if I did have any money, I wouldn't give it to you."

The man turned away as if to go back inside the Salty Dog.

Strate grabbed his shirt and jerked him back. "You didn't let me finish," Strate said. "You didn't let me tell you what was going to happen to you if you didn't tell me about Patch."

The man tried to pull away, but Strate twisted his hand in the shirt and held on.

"I don't know nothin'," the man rasped. "I was tryin' to make some money."

Strate lowered his head until his mouth was right by the man's ear. "Then you sure did go about it in the wrong way," he whispered. "You lied to the wrong man, and now I'm going to throw you out there in that street and see how long you can breathe with your face buried in six inches of mud."

The man writhed in Strate's grip, but he couldn't free himself. "Let go," he said, panting with the effort.

Strate didn't say anything, just began to drag the man to the edge of the porch. The man tried to kick, but his feet slipped out from under him. Strate prepared to heave him in the mud, keeping his grip on the shirt with one hand and grabbing the seat of the man's pants with the other.

"Wait," the man said.

"Why?" Strate said.

"I'll tell you," the man said.

Strate pulled him upright. "Make it quick. My friend's getting wet out there."

"I don't know all that much. I don't even really know Patch all that well, but I heard he was in town. You hear things when you sit around in places like this a lot."

"I know he's in town," Strate said. "I want to know how to find him."

"Hell, I don't know that."

Strate threw him off the porch and jumped down in the mud beside him, putting his hand on the back of his head and pressing down. The cords in the man's neck stood out as he strained to keep his face out of the mud.

"I don't know where he is, I tell you," the man said. "Don't push my face in that stuff!"

Strate forced the man's head down until his face was less than an inch from the slimy street.

"I heard somebody say he might be with the Colonel," the man said. The desperation was plain in his voice.

Strate had forgotten about the Colonel. "There might be more than one colonel in a town this size," he said. "That's not much of a help."

"There's just one colonel that Patch knows."

Strate allowed the man to raise his head a fraction of an inch. "Who?"

"Colonel Benson," the man said.

"Let's go have us a drink," Strate said. He pulled the man up. "I have just about enough money for all three of us to have a whiskey." He looked up at Jack. "You want one, don't you?"

"Sure do," Jack said.

"Not in there," the man said, looking behind him at the entrance to the Salty Dog.

"There's always another place to have a drink," Strate said. "Let's find it."

They found the Oyster, which made the Salty Dog look almost wholesome. That was fine with Strate, since the three of them could never have gone in anywhere respectable. He and the stooped man, whose name was Whit Barney, were covered with mud, and Jack was as wet as if he had been for a swim in all his clothes.

With the drink Barney became talkative. Colonel Benson wasn't really a colonel. He was a man who had taken that rank for himself, or so the stories went. During the war he had risen no higher than private, but the war had never really ended for him. He hated the Yankees with a passion that was hard even for other rabid Southerners to comprehend, and he had continued to wage his own private war for years after Appomattox. It was as if Lee had never surrendered. He had taken to himself the rank of colonel and continued to raid and plunder wherever and whenever he could in the Northern states, and when things had finally gotten too hot for him, he had headed for Texas.

"He 'specially hates niggers," Barney said.

Strate glanced at Jack, who might have been carved out of stone for all the sign he gave of having heard.

"What about Tollie, then?" Strate said. "He seems to be Patch's partner."

"They all fought together after the war," Barney said. "Seems like Tollie hated the Yankees as much as the Colonel did. They murdered his mama and daddy."

"Why?" Strate asked.

"I heard they fought on the side of their owner when the soldiers came through. Tried to defend his house or some such. Got shot all to hell. Tollie got away."

That would explain it, Strate thought. "Where would I find this Colonel Benson?" he asked.

"Kempton Hotel," Barney said. "Any chance of gettin' another drink?"

"No," Strate said. "Not a chance."

Chapter Four

Colonel Peter Benson watched the mosquito walk across the back of his left hand.

The mosquito was black and bloated, almost awkward in its movements because of the amount of blood it had drunk.

It had not drunk the blood from Benson's hand, however; that would have been impossible. The hand was made of solid wood, the fingers and thumb slightly curved, as if the hand were gripping something lightly. It was made of hard, polished Texas oak, and the carver had been at some pains to make it look realistic. Its knuckles stood up, and the tendons ran from them down the back of the hand to where it disappeared inside the cuff of Benson's jacket.

There were a number of stories about how Benson had lost the hand. He liked to say that it had been hacked off by a Union saber at the Battle of Gettysburg, though others said it had been amputated by some quack doctor after the palm had been pierced by a bullet when Benson had been nearly caught in the act of horse theft by a picket guard. The truth was that his hand had indeed been amputated, and by a quack, but not because Benson had been shot. He had passed out drunk near his camp one night, and a horse had stepped on him, mangling the hand almost beyond recognition.

For a while Benson had contemplated wearing a hook,

but he had met an old man who carved wooden animals and who suggested that he could carve a hand just as well. The idea appealed to Benson, and the hand was made. He had worn it ever since.

The mosquito negotiated one of the tendons before Benson reached down and crushed it with his right thumb. It did not even try to escape, being perhaps too full to attempt flight. Its frail legs separated from the body as the blood spurted out to stain the back of the hand.

Benson reached inside his jacket and extracted a handkerchief, which he flicked at the top of his hand. The various body parts of the mosquito were knocked aside before Benson began to rub at the blood.

When he was satisfied that his hand was once again clean, he looked at Patch, who was sitting uncomfortably in a straightbacked chair upholstered with green fabric.

"You had no trouble getting here, I hope," he said. His voice was deep and mellow, more the kind of voice you might expect from a music-hall entertainer than from a renegade Southerner who had spent most of his life on the wrong side of the law.

"No," Patch said. "We didn't have any trouble." Patch had long since decided that it would not be wise to tell the Colonel of their good fortune on the way to Houston. It was in the Colonel's nature to be greedy, and Patch didn't want to have to share the money he had come into with anyone. Greed was an emotion that he understood entirely, and his only regret was that he had been forced to split the money three ways already.

"The others?" Benson said.

"They're here in town. They wanted to blow off a little steam." Patch had no idea where Tollie and Seth were. He suspected that they would already be spending part of their share of the money in some whorehouse, but he wasn't going to tell the Colonel that, either.

The Colonel stood up. He had been sitting at a small wooden desk, varnished black and polished to a high sheen. When he stood, he was hardly any taller than he had been sitting down. Patch was always surprised at how short the Colonel was.

"I have a job for you, if you're interested," the Colonel said.

"We're interested," Patch told him, though it wasn't really true. They had been interested before they got the money, but now he was there only because of the Colonel. Patch would always come when the Colonel called. The Colonel had taken him out of the cotton patch and showed him how to get money the easy way—by taking it from others. It was a lesson that Patch had always appreciated and had learned well.

"I want you to kill someone," the Colonel said.

That sounded fine to Patch. "Who?" he said.

After they left the Oyster, Jack and Lee had to find a place to stay. Or, as Jack pointed out, separate places.

"It's not likely that any place where you might stay will take me," Jack said. Strate didn't have to ask him why.

There was another problem, however.

"Money," Strate said. "I don't have any. I spent my last dollar on drinks."

They were riding William aimlessly down the street, back in the direction of the better part of town. It had stopped raining, and the mosquitoes were out in force, buzzing and biting. There was a smell in the air of mud and dampness, not the clean smell that often comes after a rain in places of lower humidity and higher altitude, but an unpleasant, unhealthy smell. Strate thought of the stories he had heard of yellow fever.

"I have a little money," Jack said after a while.

They rode a little farther on William.

"I couldn't pay you back," Strate said. "Not unless we found those men and my money."

"You could get a job," Jack said.

"I guess I could do that," Strate said. The idea didn't appeal to him. He didn't want a job. He wanted his money back.

"You can't go to that hotel where that Colonel is, looking like you do," Jack said. "They'd throw you right back out the front door. You've got to clean up and look respectable if it's a nice hotel."

Strate was pretty sure it would be a nice hotel. He didn't know much about the Colonel, but he knew enough to think that the man would stay at only the best places. According to Whit Barney, the Colonel had long ago graduated from petty thievery and outlawry to bigger, it not necessarily better, things.

"He's in with the big dogs now" was the way Barney had put it. "One o' the swells. You'd never see him in this part of town." Barney had looked around the Oyster as if seeing it for the first time: the dirt on the floors, the grime on the glasses they were drinking from.

Barney didn't know what the Colonel was involved in. He heard a lot of stories when he hung around the cheap bars, but all he could say was that the Colonel "had a lot of friends in the gov'ment." Which government, Barney didn't know, and he didn't care. "The gov'ment don't give a hoot in hell about me," he said. "So I don't give a damn about them, either."

But he was sure that the Colonel had powerful friends and was making money by doing them favors. If he had called for Patch and the others, it was because he had a job for them.

"It's like I said. They was all in the war together, or anyway, they were together after it. They all rode together for quite a few years, till the Colonel got enough money to retire from the business and get respectable. But they still do jobs for him, Patch and Tollie and Seth do. I guess they didn't get as rich as he did." He shook his head. "Or as respectable."

So Strate thought that if he was going to walk into a respectable hotel, he ought to look respectable, too. Jack was clearly right about that.

"You could look at it this way," Strate told him. "It's like an investment. You let me borrow a little money now, and I'll pay you back when I get my own money. And that's on top of what your share will be."

William plodded on, his feet slopping in the mud.

"If I did do that," Jack said, "you'd have to find a hotel a little less fancy than the Kempton. I'm not willing to invest that much."

"Anywhere you say," Strate said. "You pick the place. I could use a little extra, though. You know, for food and such."

"No whiskey," Jack said.

"I wouldn't do that," Strate said. "I've already had more whiskey today than I usually drink in a month.

There was a snort of derision. Strate wasn't sure whether Jack or William was the snorter.

"How do you plan to approach the Colonel?" Jack asked.

"I wasn't planning to approach him," Strate said. "I thought I'd get me a newspaper and sit in the lobby of the hotel. Sooner or later Patch or one of the others will be by. Then I'll have a little talk with him, and that will be that."

"I don't think it will be that easy," Jack said. "What if he sees you first?"

"I'll be hiding behind the newspaper."

"What if they don't come by?"

"They'll come by. They have to." Strate wasn't as certain as he tried to sound. "If they don't, then I'll see the Colonel."

"How?"

"Don't ask so many questions!" Strate said. "You can take my word for it."

"It's my money I'm worried about, you see," Jack said. "I don't like to make an investment unless I have some assurance that I'll at least get my money back."

"All right," Strate said. "If I don't get the five thousand dollars, I'll get a job and pay you back every penny that I borrow. That's a promise."

"That's good enough for me," Jack said.

He sounded as if he meant it, but Strate wasn't sure.

*   *   *

Patch was pacing around the hotel room. He had taken his hat off and was rubbing his thick brown hair. "I didn't have any idea you'd be wanting us for something like this," he said.

The Colonel was seated at the desk, running the fingers of his right hand over the back of the wooden one. "It is quite a task, indeed," he said. "You can rely on the fact that my backers are aware of the difficulty and have put up a considerable sum of money for the job, of which you and your friends will take away your share."

Money didn't matter that much to Patch at the moment. He already had more than he had ever hoped to get in one lump, and the thought of more didn't appeal to him as much as it might have at any other time. It was the magnitude of what the Colonel had told him that had shaken him. This wasn't like stealing horses or robbing farmhands.

When Patch didn't speak, the Colonel said, "What is it that disturbs you most about the plan? You've killed men before, so it can't be that."

"It's not that," Patch said. "But this is a big operation. Are you sure that Tollie and Seth and me can handle it?"

"I wouldn't have called you otherwise," the Colonel said, lying through his teeth. He wasn't at all sure they could handle the job, and the fact that Tollie was Negro particularly disturbed him. Unfortunately a black man was one of the requirements for the job. And then there was Seth, who was almost dim-witted. He could follow orders all right, but he could never be trusted on his own. Still, these were men that the Colonel knew he could rely on to keep a secret and to do what he told them, insofar as they could. He might have wished for better men, but these were the ones he had. They would have to do.

"I hope you're right," Patch said. "Let's go over it one more time. You want us to go to Galveston tomorrow. You want Tollie to join this Cotton Jammers association, and you want me to join something called the Screwmen. Then we stir up trouble. I'm not quite straight on that. What kind of trouble?"

"You won't have to worry about that," Benson assured him. "The trouble is already there, as you'll see when you join. Your memberships have already been set up, by the way. There should be no difficulty."

"It's white against black, is that right?"

The Colonel sighed. "Let me go over it for you one more time. The two strongest labor organizations on the Galveston docks are the Screwmen and the Cotton Jammers. White and black. There is a certain amount of unrest at the present time. The whites are threatening to strike for higher wages. Many people suspect that if they do, the blacks will step in and offer to do all the jobs, thereby ending the strike and depriving the whites of their wages for quite some time to come. That is not something that I would like to see come about."

"And you really think President Grant will come to Galveston to do something about the strike?"

"I do not think it, I know it. He will be there, along with the others. Sheridan. Cuney. All of them. No one will say why. They will all call it a pleasure trip, or a political jaunt, but they will be there to try to avert the strike."

"But do we want the strike?"

"We don't really care about the strike. Our goals are elsewhere. If there could be open violence between the organizations, our purposes would be served. The more violence, the better to show the world the inherent viciousness of the black man. I would not object if there were riots. In fact, I would prefer it."

"And the . . . uh, killing?"

"You may call it an assassination if you wish. Tollie would be the ideal man to pull the trigger, but you or Seth would do nearly as well."

"I'm a little worried about Seth."

Benson did not feel that it was necessary to express his own doubts about Seth. He simply said, "Why?"

"Well, he doesn't really have a job to do."

"Don't worry about that," the Colonel said. "I'll be arriving in Galveston shortly after you, and I'm sure I can find some little jobs for him.'' Indeed, he had several things in mind, but he did not believe in telling anyone, even Patch, more than was absolutely necessary.

"All right, then," Patch said doubtfully.

"Don't worry," Benson said. "It will all work out, I assure you." He hoped he was telling the truth this time. "Now let me give you the money for your rail tickets." He opened a small drawer in the desk and took out some bills.

Strate relaxed in the hot water of the bath. Any hotel that could provide a bath was all right with him, even though it might not be nearly as fancy as the one where the Colonel was staying. He just hoped that Patch hadn't spent all the money yet, and that Tollie and Seth weren't enjoying a hot bath right at that moment at the expense of his five thousand.

He thought for a minute about Jack Farmer. He had never really known a black man before, but Jack seemed all right. He had stopped to help, and not everyone would have done that. He had even let Strate borrow enough money to stay at a hotel and have a bath. Not everyone would have done that, either. In fact, damned few would have. Of course, Jack hoped to get a good return on his money, and he would if Lee got his hands on the five thousand or what was left of it.

As the water started to cool, Strate thought about what he would do to Tollie and Patch if he got his hands on them. Not to mention that little mush-mouth who'd come creeping up on him like that and wormed his way into the camp.

Shooting was too good for them, but there was no chance he would shoot them anyway. He didn't want any trouble with the law.

What he hoped to do was simply lure them into an alley, preferably one at a time, and beat the living daylights out of them.

If he only got one of them, well, that was fine, just as long as that one could tell him where the money was.

In the years since he had left the little farm in Kansas, Strate had done more than one thing that was on the shady side, he had to admit that. It was a fact that he didn't have what you could call a clear title to that five thousand, and that there were probably those who would say that Patch had as much right to it as Strate did.

But Strate didn't look at it that way.

No, he had done a job for which he had expected to be paid. The job had involved the recovery of a large sum of money stolen in a bank robbery, several times more than the five thousand that Strate expected as his reward if he made the recovery.

He had gotten the money back, but it had not been easy. He had nearly been killed more than once, and he had even suffered through a tornado.

Then, when he got the money back and it was all safely deposited in the bank again, they told him thanks and wished him a pleasant trip to wherever it was that he was going.

No mention of the money he was to get as his reward, just good wishes and a hearty handshake.

He had shaken their hands and smiled at them, all the time wondering how they thought they could get away with cheating him like that, and then he left.

At least they thought he left. When the bank was robbed a week or so later, with the robber taking only five thousand dollars, he was supposed to have been long gone.

No one would have dreamed of pinning the robbery on Lee Strate, who didn't think of it as a robbery in the first place. As far as he was concerned, he was just collecting an overdue bill.

And now somebody had collected it from him. Well, they weren't going to keep it.

He got out of the tin tub and toweled dry. He would have himself something to eat, and then he would pay a visit to the Kempton Hotel.

Chapter Five

They saw Strate first.

When he thought back on it, he wondered if Jack had jinxed him. He didn't really believe in jinxes, but it was Jack who had asked him what he would do if they saw him first.

He was pretty sure the newspaper idea would have worked, but the fact was that he never got to try it. They spotted him before he got to the Kempton Hotel.

He felt good because he was cleaner than he had been for a considerable time, dressed in clean clothes and ready to face up to Patch about the money. He wasn't even really looking at the people on the street.

It was late afternoon, a little before suppertime, and the streets were nearly clear. The clouds had not cleared away entirely, but there were little patches of blue here and there. It was still muggy, and the heavy smell of dampness was still in the air.

Strate had picked up a newspaper in the lobby of his own hotel and was carrying it rolled up under his arm. He wasn't going to start reading it until he got to the Kempton. He wasn't really interested in the Houston news.

He was walking briskly along, pausing to consider at every street the driest way to cross. He had cleaned his boots carefully, and he didn't want to get them any muddier than he had to.

Tollie and Seth walked right into him, nearly knocking him down. They had been coming down a side street, talking and laughing about something they had said or done in a bar, not particularly watching where they were walking. They thought that if someone didn't want to get walked on, he could move over.

Strate didn't move, because he didn't really see or hear them. He was looking at an especially muddy spot in the middle of the street, a spot that might have qualified as a lake in some of the drier parts of West Texas, and wondering how he could bypass it.

When they collided with him, he was knocked sideways slightly, and Tollie reached out to grab his arm and steady him.

"What the hell," Strate said, looking at the two men. Then he recognized them.

The rolled-up newspaper dropped from under his right arm as he went for his gun.

Seth's eyes widened. "It's him!" he yelled.

Tollie may or may not have known who Seth meant, but both of them turned and ran back in the direction from which they had come.

Strate had heard a good deal about Houston from Jack as they had made their journey there. He knew that the number of shootings and murders there was about as high as anywhere in the country, or at least that's what Jack had said.

Still, he didn't want to risk firing off his pistol right there on the main street. There weren't many people out and about, but there was always the chance that he would hit one of them, and he didn't want that.

And he didn't want to attract the attention of the law. He knew that the five thousand dollars was his, but there was no way he could really prove it. He didn't want any inquisitive lawman asking him too much about where the money had come from, either. It wasn't anything that he wanted to try to explain.

So he holstered the Peacemaker and went after them.

They turned left into the first alley they passed.

Strate cursed. So much for the bath and the clean clothes.

He stopped at the entrance to the alley. It was between two tall buildings, both of them three stories high. The blue patches of sky were turning to gray, and the sun was sinking lower every minute. The alley was dark and full of shadows.

Strate waited until he was breathing normally again, and then drew his pistol. He had no way of knowing whether the alley led on to another street or whether it was a dead end. Either way, Tollie and Mush-mouth could be waiting in there for him.

He leveled the pistol and stepped into the mud, feeling his boots sink into it about an inch.

The other end of the alley was open. In the shadows along the side of the building on the right there was a hooped barrel, and on the left there was a stack of crates.

Keeping the pistol ready, Strate started down the alley.

When he came to the barrel, he looked inside. Its sides were wet, and it was full of rainwater. He moved away.

"Now!" someone yelled.

Strate heard the sound of water rushing out of the barrel, and he wheeled around to see Seth rising from the barrel, a stick in his hands.

Strate fired his pistol, but he was still turning; the shot went wild.

Seth hit him with the stick. It connected solidly with Strate's left shoulder, and the pain shot down his arm. He held on to the pistol and tried to raise it to fire again.

He got the shot off at just about the same instant that Tollie hit him in the back, driving him forward into the barrel. The bullet smacked into the mud, followed closely by the Peacemaker, just before Strate crashed into the barrel.

Tollie had rammed him hard and had not let up. Strate hit the barrel full force and smashed it into the wall.

The barrel staves crushed inward, the hoops collapsed, and water gushed out over Strate.

Seth was yelling in his mush-mouthed way that they were killing him. He was in fact probably hurt more than Strate, since he was between Strate and the wall.

Strate thought that killing him was a fine idea, and he got his hands up and closed them around Seth's head. He was trying to bang it into the brick wall behind it when Tollie's hands clamped over his wrists, dragging his hands down.

Seth was still yelling, and now he began shaking his head like a dog, flinging drops of water in every direction from the tips of his soaking hair. He was still trapped in the remains of the barrel, and he was kicking at the staves and hoops, trying to free himself.

Meanwhile, Strate was stomping down backward, trying without much success to crush Tollie's foot. His own feet kept slipping in the mud, and then he went down, dragging Tollie with him.

Somehow Seth managed to fall right on top of them, hoops, staves, and all. He immediately started trying to butt Strate on the chin with the top of his head.

Tollie was still holding Strate's wrists, and there was nothing Strate could do about Seth except try to kick him off. Somehow he got a knee up and into Seth's midsection and shoved, sending Seth over into the mud on his back.

Tollie let go of Strate's wrists then and got an arm lock around Strate's throat.

Suddenly Strate found himself unable to breathe. He got his hands on Tollie's arm and began to pull, but the arm was like iron and impossible to budge. Strate could feel his face getting hot, and he knew he was turning red, though his color was the least of his worries.

What he had to worry about was breathing.

He let go of Tollie's arm and reached higher, looking for a more sensitive portion of the black man's anatomy. Reaching behind his own head, he felt Tollie's face.

He couldn't get his fingers into Tollie's nostrils, but he did get his thumbs into his eyes and began pressing down as hard as he could. If he could pop them right out, he would be happy.

Tollie screamed, and Strate felt the pressure relax on his neck. He sat up, and Seth flew into him, butting him squarely in the center of the chest.

Strate slid off Tollie and backward through the mud.

He was struggling to get up when Tollie kicked him. Hadn't all this happened to him before?

"Kill him, Tollie," Seth said mushily. "We should've killed him the last time, 'stead of just takin' his money."

"I do believe you're right," Tollie said, reaching for his gun.

Strate heard three shots. His body jerked in anticipation of the bullets striking his flesh, but nothing like that happened. Instead the bullets hit the brick wall high above him and whined off into the distance.

Tollie and Seth ran off down the alley, their boots squelching through the mud.

Strate sat up and looked to the entrance of the alley. There was a man walking toward him. The man was holding a smoking revolver in one hand. It was too dark to make out the man's features, but Strate could tell that he was carrying plenty of bulk.

The man approached Strate and reached down to grab his arm. As he pulled Strate to his feet he said, "This damn town's gettin' to be more dangerous than the army. Nothin' but a nest of damn thieves and robbers."

Strate agreed with him and tried to brush some of the mud off his clothes. It was too sticky to do much with, however.

"Lucky for you I heard those shots," the man said.

Strate agreed with him again and began looking around in the mud for his pistol. He found it and picked it up. He was sure there was mud in the barrel and that it would need a good cleaning.

"They get away with anything?" the man asked.

Strate was sure they hadn't. There hadn't been time, and he didn't have anything for them to take. But he patted himself down, anyway.

"Not this time," he said.

"This time? You been robbed already today?"

"Not today," Strate said. "But not too long ago." He didn't say more. He didn't want to have to explain himself to the bulky man.

"Damn," the man said. "Robbed twice, and right in

downtown Houston. It's like I say, mister, the damn robbers are takin' over the town. That's why I came down the alley. Not ever'body in town would've done that—scared they'd get their ears shot off.''

"I appreciate you showing up," Strate said. "They had the drop on me for sure."

"It don't do to go walkin' down alleys," the man said. "You never know what you might run into."

Strate started to tell him that he hadn't walked down the alley, but then he thought better of it. Let the man think what he wanted to. He reached into his pocket and fished around for some of Jack's money.

"I'd like to buy you a drink," he said. "I can't go to a bar with you, not looking like I do, but you can have one on me."

The man shook his head. "No thanks. I just like to do my part to help out a fella when he's got trouble." He stuck out a hand and Strate shook it. Then he turned to leave.

"Thanks again," Strate called after him.

"Don't mention it," the man said. "Glad to help out."

Strate watched the man's dark bulk walk down the alley and turn left. For the second time recently, Strate had been helped out in a time of trouble by someone who had nothing to gain by doing so. It was enough to make a man think. Ever since leaving the farm, Strate had been on his own and doing pretty well. He hadn't given much consideration to other people and their feelings, and he damn sure hadn't ever stopped to help out someone in trouble. He'd been concerned mainly with himself.

Well, there was nothing wrong with that. If he wanted his money back, who was to say that was wrong? And he was willing to give Jack a good share of it when the time came. He had to admit that if their situations had been reversed and Jack were the one needing the money and the help, he might not have been so willing to respond, but that didn't mean there was anything wrong with him.

After he got his five thousand back, then he'd take time to help someone else. Maybe. He'd worry about that when the time came.

He limped out of the alley, covered in mud, his shoulder aching, his neck sore.

He hoped that he had enough of Jack's money left to pay for another bath.

Tollie and Seth had been planning to meet Patch in front of the Kempton. Though there were some places where whites and blacks could mingle in Houston, they were places like the Oyster, not the lobby of the Kempton Hotel. Even Seth would have looked seedy and out of place there.

Patch was different. He had the ability to dress the part of the swell, and his black patch, instead of making him look disreputable, gave him the air of a distinguished gentleman who had suffered a devastating wound in battle. He could go in and out of the finest places, if he chose to, without raising the suspicions of the most punctilious desk clerk.

Because of the fight in the alley, Tollie and Seth could not even wait in front of the hotel. It would have been only a matter of time before some officer of the law spotted them and wondered why two such mud-covered vagrants were lurking around a fine establishment like the Kempton.

So they hid in an alley across the street, watching the hotel entrance carefully so that they would not miss Patch when he came out into the street.

When they spotted him, Seth put his fingers into his mouth and gave a piercing whistle.

It was early evening now, and a soft darkness was settling on the city, but Patch knew the whistle and could make out the two figures waving to him from across the street. He made his way across to them.

Seth didn't give Patch a chance to ask what had happened. He started immediately to tell him.

"We ran right into the son of a bitch," he said. "Practically knocked him down on the walk!" When he got excited, Seth tended to get even more mush-mouthed than usual, and to spray his listener with spit if he got too close.

Patch backed away, wiping at his face with his hand. "Slow down," he said. "What son of a bitch are you talking about?"

"The one—the one—the one—"

Seth was too worked up to talk about it. Tollie put his hand on the little man's shoulder, and Seth hushed.

"The one whose camp we rode up on the other day," Tollie said. "The one whose money we took."

"He's here in Houston?" Patch didn't like this development. It might have a bearing on their job in Galveston.

"He's here, all right," Tollie said.

"We shoulda—shoulda—" Seth said.

"Killed him the first time," Tollie finished for him.

"Did you kill him this time?" Patch asked.

"We started—started—"

"Someone interrupted us," Tollie explained. "We had the drop on him, but somebody came up on us and started shooting. We got out of there."

"That might mean he's got a partner," Patch said. He was liking it less and less.

"It might be all right," Tollie said. "Running into him was just an accident. He doesn't know why we're here, or what we're going to do. If we just stay out of sight, we won't see him again."

"Maybe," Patch said. He thought about it. "You're probably right. Anyway, we'll be leaving for Galveston tomorrow. He won't know about that, and he won't follow us there."

"What are we gonna do in Galveston?" Seth wanted to know. He had calmed down and could speak coherently once again. "Is it a job for the Colonel?"

"That's what it is," Patch said.

Then he told them about the job.

Chapter Six

All the next day Strate waited in the hotel lobby, reading the newspaper that he held in front of his face as he sat on first a divan, then on an overstuffed chair, then on the divan again. He had read all the items in the newspaper ten or twelve times. He practically had them memorized, which wasn't easy, considering that he had looked up after nearly every sentence to watch the comings and goings in the lobby.

He didn't see a single person that he recognized, not Patch, not either of the other two.

He could hardly believe it. The day before, they had practically trampled him on the sidewalk. Today, not a one of them had come near the hotel, or at least they hadn't come inside it.

The lobby was spacious, but he had been able to watch all of it, and by careful changing of his position he had avoided the suspicions of the desk clerks, or so he hoped. It had all been for nothing, however. The men he wanted had not showed up.

He thought about going to the desk and asking for Colonel Stuart Benson, but he didn't want to call attention to himself any more than he had so far, and he suspected that the Colonel would not see him, anyway. Or if he did see him, that he would not be sympathetic to his complaint.

There was nothing to do but call it a day and try again tomorrow. He was very hungry, not having left the lobby even to eat, and he might have tried staying even later had his stomach not been gnawing at his backbone. It was already nearly dark outside, and if no one had come by now, no one was coming. Or so he believed.

He went out for a quick meal, and then, instead of going to his own room as he had planned, he returned to the Kempton. He waited for three more hours, but there was no sign of the men he was looking for.

Discouraged, he returned to his own hotel to wait until morning. He was sure that Tollie and the other one had been heading for the Kempton the day before. Why not today? And where had Patch been? Had he already met with the mysterious Colonel?

The answers to the questions didn't really matter one way or the other. He would simply have to try again.

The next day, however, was even more frustrating. There was not only no sign of the three men, but the desk clerk was showing definite signs of curiosity, a dangerous situation that was only one step away from his either calling the law or at least demanding to know who Strate was and what he thought he was doing in the lobby of such a fine hotel.

Just before dark, Strate decided to take the initiative. He had been more or less concealing himself behind a thick column for over an hour, and he hoped that the clerk had forgotten him. He laid his newspaper on a chair and walked over to the desk.

"I'm here to see Colonel Benson," he announced to the clerk.

The clerk, a mousy little man with slicked-down hair and a pointy nose, looked at Strate with disbelief. "Are you?" he said.

"That's right," Strate said. "I have an appointment to meet him here at this hotel. This is the Kempton, isn't it?"

"Of course it is," the clerk said. He had a little of the north in his accent, and Strate wondered where he had come from. "What time was your appointment?"

"Right about now," Strate said. He didn't own a watch.

"You're sure about that?"

There was something about the clerk's tone that Strate didn't like, but he said, "I'm sure."

"I'll just bet you are," the clerk said, openly sneering.

"Look here," Strate said. "I want you to tell me the Colonel's room number. He'll be mighty upset if I'm late."

"Somehow I doubt that."

Strate had noticed before that there were certain times when people were more apt to put on airs than others. One of those times was when they were sure they had the upper hand.

"Isn't he here?" Strate said.

"Of course not," the clerk said. "As you would well know, if you really had an appointment to see him. He checked out this morning."

Strate did not try to think of a snappy reply. He simply turned from the desk and walked out. When he got to the doorway, he looked back, but the clerk had already forgotten about him and turned to other tasks. To him, Strate was just another faker trying to bluff his way into the presence of one of the hotel's guests. Not someone worth worrying about.

Strate went out into the heavy darkness. It wasn't raining, but it felt as if there were enough moisture in the air to rain at any second. He swiped idly at a mosquito that flew in front of his face, making a thin, high-pitched whine.

"Strate."

He looked up at the sound of his name. Jack Farmer was standing at his elbow.

"You ought to watch where you're going," Jack said.

Strate thought about his encounter with Tollie and Seth. "That's the truth," he said. "Did you come all the way here to tell me that?"

"No," Jack said. "I came to tell you that you're wasting your time in that hotel."

Strate swatted at the mosquito again. Or maybe it was a different one. "That's the truth, too. How'd you know?"

"I'se the sebenth son of a sebenth son."

Strate looked at him. "You're talking that way again," he said. "And I don't believe in that hoodoo stuff."

"There might be more to it than you think," Jack said. "That's not really how I know, however."

"I didn't think so."

"As it happens, the son of a cousin of mine works in that hotel. Did I tell you that I was staying with my cousin?"

"No. You just said you knew a place where you could stay and not have to spend much money."

"That's my cousin's. The bed isn't very comfortable, but it's free. I happened to mention to him tonight over supper that you were looking for some men in the vicinity of the Kempton."

The mention of supper made Strate's stomach growl.

Jack ignored the rumble. "His son was there eating with us. He was curious and asked which men I was referring to. I told him about Colonel Benson, and he said that the Colonel had checked out early this morning."

Strate thought about the traffic in the lobby. He had been looking for people coming in, not people checking out, but he had naturally noticed some of those who had left that day. There hadn't been many, and only one of them could have been the Colonel.

"Little fella," Strate said. "But carries himself stiff and straight as a poker."

"That's the one," Jack said. "Did you know that he has a wooden hand?"

"Wood?"

"Something happened to the real one. He got him a wooden one, carved just like the one he lost."

"You happen to know where he went?"

"Galveston," Jack said.

Strate went to the hotel for his things. He was going to spend the night with Jack at the house of Jack's cousin, who was going to tell him all about Galveston.

It wasn't much of a house—more of a shanty, really—located among rows of similar shanties of the same approximate size and shape in what was a sort of freedman's town near the main section of the city. The streets here were narrower and muddier, if that was possible, than those Strate had already seen, and he felt vaguely uncomfortable as he trudged along beside Jack. He could see the curtains move on lamplit windows as they walked by the houses, and black children in the muddy yards stopped their play to watch them pass in the night.

Strate mentioned his feelings to Jack.

"Don't feel bad about it," Jack said. "I feel that way most of the time."

"Here?" Strate said.

"No," Jack said. "Back where we came from."

Jack's cousin, whose name was Aaron, was uncomfortable as well. He didn't like the idea of having a white man in his house.

"I appreciate that you're a friend of Jack's," he said when they got there. "But all the same, we don't see many white faces in this part of town."

Aaron had a wife, Sarah, and two children whose names Strate never learned. They hid behind their mother's skirts and peered out at Strate as if he were some kind of circus freak. He thought that to them, he probably was. Although he stayed in the house overnight, they never overcame their shyness enough to speak to him or even get close to him.

For that matter, neither did Sarah. She served them their evening meal of rice, red beans, and corn bread without saying a word.

Strate did not try to draw her or the children out. He understood that they were feeling awkward and probably wondering what the neighbors were thinking about the white man in the house. Besides, his main interest was not in trying to make friends. He wanted to find out something about Galveston, the city to which Colonel Benson had gone.

"First of all," Aaron said, biting off a hefty hunk of corn bread, "it's an island, if you can call it that." He chewed.

"If it's not an island, what is it?" Strate asked. He wasn't comfortable with the idea of an island in the first place. He had seen the ocean, but he had seen it from the shore. He didn't like the thought of being on a parcel of land that wasn't connected to anything and was surrounded with lots of water. It occurred to him that, living in Kansas as he had for most of his life, he had never learned to swim.

"It's more like a sandbar," Aaron said. "It just barely sticks up out of the water enough to call it anything at all. It's a wonder to me that the waves don't just wash right over it." He dished himself up another helping of beans.

Strate was rapidly losing his appetite. Galveston didn't sound like a place that he wanted to go in the least.

"It's really not that bad," Jack said, noticing Strate's look. "Plenty of people live there. It's one of the biggest cities in the state, and by far the most civilized."

Strate was getting confused. "Is it a city or an island?"

"Both," Jack said. "The city is named Galveston, and it's on the island of Galveston. The city doesn't cover the whole island, though. Just a part of it."

"Long time back, they called it the Island of the Snakes," Aaron said. "Lots of rattlers down there. You'd best watch your step, even in town."

Strate didn't like snakes any more than he liked islands. In fact, he probably liked snakes even less. "I don't see how a town got started there," he said.

"People live anywhere," Aaron said. "For a long time pirates lived there, but it's not that way now."

"Aaron used to work down there," Jack said. "They moved back up here to be close to Sarah's family. Her daddy's not in good health."

"Worked on the docks," Aaron said. "I was one of the Cotton Jammers." There was a note of pride in his voice.

"Cotton Jammers?" Strate said. "What's a Cotton Jammer?"

"Fella that jams cotton," Aaron said.

"Where did you jam it?"

"Ships. That's what Galveston is all about. Ships. They come in there loaded with one thing, and they go out loaded with something else. Mostly cotton. Trouble is, those cotton bales that come from the compresses are so big and loose that you can't get as many of them in the hold as the bosses would like. So we'd jam in more."

"How could you do that?" Strate said.

"We had these big jackscrews," Aaron said. "You get that cotton in the hold and mash it down tight with those screws. Then you jam in some more. It takes a strong man to work in those gangs, let me tell you." He pulled up the sleeve of his shirt and showed Strate his thick, corded arm. "Wrestling those bales over to the ship from the warehouse is tough, too. It wasn't that we could get a lot more cotton on board, but we got enough on there so the owners could make a little more money. They paid us good, too." There was as much wistfulness as pride in his voice now, and Strate guessed that he was not doing as well in Houston.

"There's some trouble on the docks down there now, I hear," Aaron went on. "Some folks say there's going to be a strike by the white workers. I don't know anything about that, though. They run a closed shop, call themselves the Screwmen. No black men allowed."

All that was interesting information, but Strate wasn't sure that it would help him find the Colonel. And he wasn't sure that if he found the Colonel, he would find Patch. Once again, however, he felt that he was left with no other options. If the Colonel was in Galveston, Patch had to be there as well. If not, good-bye to the five thousand dollars.

"How do I get to this island?" Strate said.

"Train," Aaron said. "Or you could go by boat."

"That would cost money," Strate said flatly. "Either way." He had been hoping that he might be able to ride over on William if there was a bridge.

"Jack tells me you got plenty of money," Aaron said.

"I had plenty," Strate said. "I don't have it now."

"You think you'll ever get it back?" Aaron asked.

"It's beginning to look like I might not," Strate said. "And I'm beginning to wonder if it's worth the trouble."

"That much money is worth a world of trouble, if you ask me," Aaron said. "Nobody asked me, though."

Strate looked at Jack. It was very warm in the room, and the light from the single lamp was dim. Strate couldn't read

Jack's expression. "You got me to Houston," he said. "You even loaned me some money that you didn't have to loan. I already owe you."

"That's true," Jack said. "You do."

"I hate to give up on this," Strate said.

"I can see that you would," Jack told him. "A man starts something, he likes to finish it."

"That's right. It's more than just the money now. If it was just that, I might let it go. But I feel like I've gone too far for that. I want some satisfaction."

"They might've spent all your money by now," Aaron said.

"I don't think so," Strate said. "They'd have to be spending it mighty fast."

"I'm like you," Jack said. "I've come this far, so if I'm going to get any return on my investment, I'll have to go a little farther."

"How far are you willing to go?" Strate said.

"I might be willing to go as far as Galveston."

"Might be?"

"I might need more of a return. My investment keeps getting bigger."

"I've been thinking about that," Strate said. "I'll give you half."

"That surely sounds fair," Jack said. "I'll take it."

"I don't mean half of five thousand," Strate said. "I mean half of whatever we get back. I'm not so sure we'll get anything, not now."

"I'm willing to take the chance," Jack said. "Even half is a lot of money to me." He looked at his cousin. "Of course, we'll be willing to pay you something for your help."

"That's right," Strate said.

"I haven't done anything," Aaron said.

"You've told me a lot I didn't know," Strate said. "You've fed me and given me a place to stay."

"I could use the money," Aaron said. "Sarah's daddy. . . ."

"You'll get a share, then," Strate said.

"Out of both our halves," Jack said.

"That seems fair," Strate agreed.

Strate didn't sleep well that night. His restlessness had nothing to do with the thin quilt he was using as a pallet, the hard floor on which the pallet lay, or the damp heat that caused his clothes to stick to him. He was troubled instead by worries about the money, the Colonel, and the island of Galveston.

What if he got to the island and couldn't find the Colonel or Patch? What if the Colonel had sailed for parts unknown, and Patch and the others were riding happily to San Antonio or Dallas to spend Strate's money? Why couldn't he just let the whole thing go?

The last question didn't really bother him as much as the others. He'd been shot and beaten, and he wanted to do something about it whether he got the money back or not. His father would have called it stubbornness. His brothers would have called it pride. It was probably both, but whatever it was, it was undeniably there. There wasn't a thing he could do about it.

After he realized that, a couple of hours before dawn, he finally went to sleep.

Chapter Seven

It was raining when Strate took the train from Houston to Galveston. He wouldn't have minded so much if the car in which he was riding hadn't leaked, but the rain was coming down in sheets and forcing its way through cracks in the roof and side of the car. He could see it dripping onto the hat of a woman three seats in front of him. She didn't seem to notice, and he didn't bother to call it to her attention.

In one way he was glad of the rain, uncomfortable though it was. It was raining so hard that he could hardly see the bay when the train passed over it. Water washed over the outside of the window and changed the sky and sea into one gray haze. He couldn't tell where one ended and the other began.

He could tell from the sound of the train when it left the solid ground of the mainland and got onto the bridge, but that didn't bother him as much as it might have had he been able to see.

When the train pulled into the Galveston depot, he got off and went to look for Jack, who had not been able to ride in the same car.

"You have any cousins here you can stay with?" Strate asked.

"As a matter of fact, I do," Jack said.

They walked out into the street. It had stopped raining

again. Strate was having trouble getting used to the rapid weather changes on the coast.

The streets of Galveston appeared to be quite different from those of Houston. They were paved with tar-covered wooden blocks, and there were also paved sidewalks. The streets were busy with people, pedestrians, bicycle riders, carriage drivers. Strate saw a horse-drawn streetcar in the distance.

The people were dressed different from the Houstonians, too. They looked to Strate as if they were dressed for church. He felt almost self-conscious in his Levi's. And he was the only one around wearing a pistol.

"This is a fancy place," he said.

"Right over there is the Strand," Jack said, pointing. "They call it that after some street in England."

Strate looked in the direction Jack indicated. There were buildings that rivaled those in Houston in height but that were somehow more graceful in appearance.

"The docks aren't far," Jack said. "You can see the masts of the ships."

He was right, Strate could see the masts sticking up over the tops of the buildings in the distance.

"What's that smell?" Strate asked.

Jack took a deep breath. "Salt air. Maybe a few dead fish. Lots of things. That's just the way it smells down here."

A boy walked up to them. He was dressed in ragged clothes and wore a tattered cap. "Wanna see the light?" he said.

"What light?" Strate asked. He looked around him. The gray sky showed no signs of letting the sun break through.

"The 'lectric light."

Strate had no idea what the boy was talking about. He looked at Jack.

"It's a new invention," Jack said. "It uses electricity to produce light. It's like a gaslight, but safer."

"That's right," the boy said. "You can ride the trolley down to the beach and see it at the 'lectric Pavilion. It just costs a penny to look."

Strate shook his head. "Maybe later."

The boy moved on, looking for someone else to persuade.

"You might really want to look at that light," Jack said. "It's the kind of thing that everyone wants to see."

He had a point, Strate thought. Later he would take a look and watch the crowd, if there was one. Besides, he wanted to see the beach.

They moved off through the crowd, carrying the small bundles of their belongings.

"What kind of place does your cousin have?" Strate asked. He had an idea that he might be able to stay there with Jack and save the cost of a hotel.

"It's a sizable place," Jack said, "but I don't think you'd be welcome there. It's a whorehouse."

"A whorehouse?"

"This is a seaport town," Jack said. "Haven't you ever heard about sailors?"

Strate had heard.

"They don't like for the blacks and whites to mix," Jack said. "Not even at the whorehouses."

"I don't want to cause any trouble," Strate said. "Not until I find Patch."

"I wish I knew what that Tollie looks like," Jack said. "You never can tell who might turn up at a whorehouse."

Strate described Tollie as well as he could. "It was dark and I didn't get a very good look at him," he said. "Then, when I bumped into him in Houston, he ran away so fast that I still didn't get to see him very well."

"He might tell one of the girls his name," Jack said. "I'll tell them to be watching."

"How often do you come down this way?" Strate asked.

"Not very often. This is the first time in a few years." He gave Strate an address on Postoffice Street. "That's where I'll be. Let's find you a hotel before I go."

The hotel was cheap but clean, located not too far off Postoffice Street. Strate sat on his bed and tried to figure out how to find either Patch or the Colonel. He figured that if he could find the latter, he could find the former.

He went down to the lobby of the hotel and picked up a copy of the *Galveston News*. The headline on the front page told him that former President U. S. Grant would soon be visiting the city, along with Philip Sheridan, who had served as Grant's lieutenant in the Civil War.

There was no reason that Patch's trip to Galveston should have anything to do with Grant's visit, but Strate could not help thinking of the remark made by Barney at the Oyster. "They all fought together in the war."

It was the war that had made Grant president, and it was the war that had brought Colonel Benson together with Patch and his friends.

Strate dismissed the whole thing as coincidence. There was no way that someone like Patch, a common thief, would have anything to do with the president of the United States.

Another article on the front page pointed out the likelihood of a dock strike by the Screwmen. "It is rumored that Norris Cuney is rallying the Negro members of the Cotton Jammers to act as strikebreakers in the unlikely event that work on the docks does come to a halt," the paper said. "Should the Negro workers get the upper hand, one wonders what economic conditions in the city will be like in the future."

Strate gathered that the writer hoped the strike would never occur. The idea of Negroes getting the upper hand did not seem to appeal to him.

One of the dock owners was quoted as saying that a strike would be disastrous for the city and simply could not be allowed. Strate took that as a threat that the blacks would surely be used to defy the white workers. It sounded like a volatile situation.

There was nothing else in the paper to interest Strate, and nothing that seemed likely to give him a clue as to anyone's whereabouts. There was nothing to do except to check the hotels to see if the Colonel was registered. Then Strate could try his newspaper-reading trick again and hope it would work better than it had in Houston.

And he was going to be more watchful on the streets. He wasn't going to take the chance of getting stepped on by

Tollie and his mush-mouthed friend again without taking immediate action.

He left the lobby and went into the street. He could smell the mingled coastal smells and feel the strong Gulf breeze. He was not more than a few blocks from the water, he guessed, though he could not see it from where he was. There were too many houses in the way. Otherwise he might have been able to see it easily, since the island was so low and flat.

Oddly enough, he didn't feel as uncomfortable as he had expected he might, being on the island. Probably that was because he couldn't see the water, though it seemed to him that he could hear the waves washing up on the beach. That didn't seem likely, however. The air here was even more humid than it had been in Houston, but the breeze seemed to relieve things slightly. He had slept with the windows open all night, despite the mosquitoes, to take advantage of the wind's cooling powers.

There was no one named Benson registered in his own hotel, but then he hadn't expected that. It wasn't the sort of place where he imagined the Colonel would stay, not being nearly as classy as the Kempton, so Strate thought he would walk over to the whorehouse and find out if Jack had heard anything about Tollie. After that he would start looking for Benson in the other hotels on the island.

Tollie didn't like working on the docks. He could do the work just fine, though it was rigorous, but manhandling the heavy cotton bales was tough, even when working with a five-man team. They had to trundle the bales out of the warehouse and over to the ships, then work them into the holds.

Jamming was the right way to describe the work, all right. The first bales would go into the ship easily enough, but from there on in, things got harder. There were the jackscrews to manipulate, for one thing, and then there was the backbreaking job of forcing in more and more cotton.

The path from the warehouse to the ship was white with cotton that had dropped from the bales, and there were flecks of cotton in Tollie's hair. His shirtless black chest glistened with sweat, and bits of cotton clung to him here and there. He no longer even tried to brush it off. He was beginning to wish that he had never gotten this job, and he had been doing it for only one day. There were a great many people in the city of Galveston, he knew, who would have liked to have the job more than he did, and they gladly would have waited months to get it. Thanks to the Colonel's connections, he had not had to wait at all. The job had been waiting for him.

What he felt about the job didn't matter, though. It was what the Colonel wanted him to do, so he would do it. They had been through a lot together, and even if he had the feeling the Colonel didn't really trust him completely, they had gotten used to each other. And Tollie certainly had no objection to stirring up trouble, what with Grant coming to the city. Grant was one man that Tollie had absolutely no use for—him or Sheridan, either.

So he went about his work and didn't complain about how hard it was or how much he was sweating, even when the sweat stung his eyes and his muscles felt as if they would tear from the strain.

What he did complain about was the way he was treated in comparison to the white men who did the same work for the Screwmen. That was what Patch had told him to do.

"Let 'em know it's not fair," Patch said. "Talk to 'em about how the white men do the same job and get more money for it. That's the message the Colonel wants us to get across."

Tollie got the message. As he and the members of his team strained to further compress one of the loosely held bales, he said, "I think it's a downright shame how the white folks get more money than us for this kind of work. Man could rupture himself doin' this."

"That's right," one of the others agreed. "I've seen it happen many's the time. You take my Uncle Franklin—"

"You two hush up," Fairly Harper said. He was the team leader and the oldest of the five. His hair had so much white in it already that you couldn't tell how much of it was cotton. "We got us a good job with good wages, and we best be thankful for it."

They shoved the bale into the hold.

"That may be so," Tollie said. "Still, it don't seem fair to see the white men getting better pay.

"It sure don't," Edgar Freeman said. He was young and hot headed and likely to agree with anything contrary, just to be on the wrong side. He had arms as strong as the steel bands around the cotton. "I hear tell that the white folks might go on strike. They think they not gettin' enough pay. They oughta see what we get."

"They go on strike, that's when we could move in," Tollie said. "Get us a decent wage for what we do."

"Get our heads broke open is what we'd get," Fairly said. "Now let's us get on with this job."

Tollie didn't say any more. He knew when to talk and when to keep his mouth shut.

He also knew who to work on later. It wouldn't do to say anything else to Fairly Harper, but Edgar and the other one who'd spoken up—Thomas, his name was—those two could be cultivated when he got the chance. And he definitely intended to find the chance, some time when he was out of the way of Fairly.

It was too bad to be a man like Fairly, Tollie thought, and always be satisfied with what you had. A man ought to want to better himself, to get somewhere higher than he was, but older Fairly was willing to take whatever came his way and be grateful for it.

Tollie had learned better than that long ago.

His parents had been happy, working for Old Man Johnson on his farm, being the slaves of a white man who was no better or smarter than they were. When the soldiers came through, they had even taken up guns and fought right alongside Johnson, though by that time they were supposed to have been free.

"Free?" Tollie recalled his daddy asking him. "What's that mean, boy? You still gonna have to work for a livin', earn it by the sweat of your brow just like we always have. Marse Johnson, he's treated us right. We got plenty to eat, we got a place to stay, we got land to work. You gonna get somethin' better than that when you free?''

So the Yankees came to the farm, and Old Man Johnson tried to keep them off his land. Tollie's daddy had tried, too, just like it was *his* land they were walking on.

It didn't matter to the Yankees. They shot them both, and Tollie's mother, too. Tollie could still remember the sound the bullet made when it hit his daddy's head.

He had gotten out of there and never looked back. He knew who his enemy was then. It was anybody who tried to hurt him or keep him from what he wanted, and when he met the Colonel, he knew that he had met a man who thought the same way. They hadn't liked each other at the start, but Tollie proved that he could hate Yankees as much as any man, and the Colonel came to tolerate him and rely on him, no matter whether he trusted him or not.

And that was the funny thing, Tollie thought. He never would have dreamed of betraying the Colonel. For one reason or another, though not for any reason Tollie could explain, he actually liked Colonel Benson, liked working with him, if you could call what they did working. That was why he stuck it out on the docks, when he could easily have taken his part of the traveler's five thousand dollars and enjoyed himself for quite a long time.

He would keep working on Edgar and Thomas and any others he could find. He would try to cause enough trouble to make the Colonel proud.

Chapter Eight

There were many who had wanted President Ulysses S. Grant to serve a third term in office, despite the scandals that had plagued his second administration. Grant himself had not been one of those people, and he was actually quite relieved when the party allowed him to step aside for the nomination of Rutherford B. Hayes, who had won the election by the margin of one electoral vote.

Still, Grant's reluctance, and his two years of traveling in Europe, did nothing to diminish his popularity. In 1880, he could see that strong support was gathering for him again, but the idea of running for president did not appeal to him.

He was, however, an active man, and he was not averse to doing small political favors or jobs for the party or for his old friends. So he had not been reluctant when Hayes had called him to Washington for a talk.

They met in Grant's old office, a place that he did not miss now any more than he had for the past four years, and after the usual effusive greetings, Hayes got down to business.

"I believe you know that there are those who are going to propose your name at the convention," Hayes said. "Although I also know that you have expressed often the thought that you would rather remain a private citizen for the rest of your life."

"That is correct," Grant replied, wondering where this was leading.

Hayes nodded, his longish gray beard moving up and down. "I do not blame you one whit," he said. "Frankly I am quite happy to have decided not to run for another term. I realize, however, that my decision makes your own nomination more likely."

Grant and Hayes understood one another, in a sense. Neither had spent the best or happiest years of his life in the White House; neither wanted to spend any more years there in the future.

That was all that Grant understood, however. He still could not see where the conversation was leading them.

"I believe that I have a plan that will further both our ends," Hayes said after a pause. "It would require a little travel on your part."

Now they were getting down to business, the kind of business that Grant could understand. A favor was about to be granted, a favor that he would have to repay by some sort of journey.

"I have always liked traveling," he said. "I wonder if it could be my name."

Hayes ignored the question. "Good," he said, assuming correctly that Grant was ready to hear his proposal and likely to assent to it. "I would like for you to take a little trip down to Texas. Call it a pleasure trip, if you like. Take a friend with you, at the government's expense."

Grant nodded.

"In return I will work with all my heart to see that James Garfield receives our party's nomination to the presidency."

Hayes's motives were not entirely pure, Grant knew. Garfield was Hayes's friend and adviser, and the president would be pleased to see one of his own men nominated. Hayes had not been popular in the service of his country, but the nomination of Garfield would indicate that the party supported what Hayes had done. With the help of both Grant and Hayes, Garfield might very well achieve the goal that Hayes had in mind for him.

"I agree that Garfield is a good man," Grant said, carefully not committing himself completely. "Where would this trip take me?"

"To Texas," Hayes said. "To Galveston."

Grant knew of the island. Union troops had been quartered there during the war. But he could not think of any reason why he should go there.

"What is there in Galveston that I could do?" he asked.

"There is a bit of trouble there between two labor organizations," Hayes told him. He then explained about the Screwmen and the Cotton Jammers. "If violence breaks out, it would have far-reaching consequences. The war is slowly being forgotten. I have ended Reconstruction, and the old wounds are beginning to heal after fifteen years. But a violent confrontation, if it spread across the island, could be disastrous. There is no way to diffuse the results. The island could go up in flames."

Grant recognized the seriousness of the issue. "It could start the war all over again," he said.

"I don't believe that things would come to that," Hayes said. "But it is nevertheless a dangerous and frightening situation."

"And what would you have me do?" Grant wondered.

"Talk," Hayes said. "Even in the South, you are a man who is known and respected. Your years as president added to your stature."

Grant though he detected a note of regret in Hayes's voice. Hayes had not been nearly so popular as his predecessor, though Hayes was a thoroughly honest man who had made few of the mistakes of Grant.

"To whom would I talk?" Grant asked.

"The governor will meet with you," Hayes said. "However, the most important man for you to see will be Norris Cuney."

"I don't believe I know him."

"He is the most powerful black leader, and the most politically astute, in the state of Texas. If there are any two men who can avert this strike and its accompanying violence, you are those men. Cuney has political ambitions for himself, and some of these ambitions may be fulfilled if you and he are successful in what you attempt.''

Cuney's ambitions were exactly the opposite of Grant's, then. One of them would be a man attempting to avoid election to the highest office in the land by doing the best job he could to avert a strike in Galveston; the other would be seeking to gain political power of one kind or another, whether elective or appointive.

''I hope that you do not overestimate our abilities,'' Grant said, in essence accepting the assignment.

''I do not think so,'' Hayes said. ''There is one more thing I would tell you before you make a final decision, however.''

Grant waited.

''There are those who will be working against you,'' Hayes said.

That put a different complexion on matters, of course. It was one thing to go into a situation that might well have sad consequences when the results one hoped to gain were a matter of discussion and negotiation. It was quite another thing to enter into something that had its darker undertones.

''Exactly what do you mean to say?'' Grant asked.

''I mean that it is not simply a matter of talking to the men who control the docks and the men who control the organizations,'' Hayes said. ''I have reason to believe that there are men who are deliberately trying to create havoc, men who might not be at all sad to see happen what you mentioned earlier—the outbreak of another war.''

''Do you know which men these might be?''

''I have heard the name Benson mentioned.''

''Colonel Benson,'' Grant said thoughtfully. ''A thorn in the side of Reconstruction and all this government.''

''True,'' Hayes agreed. ''One of the worst sort, a racist who would have liked nothing better than to see the war continue indefinitely and who would like to see the black man wiped from the face of the earth.''

''As I recall,'' Grant said, ''the war never ended for him.''

Both men thought for a moment of the troubles Benson had given the government over the years. Yet he had always eluded punishment.

"I think I had heard a rumor that he was operating in Texas now," Grant said finally.

"Yes," Hayes said. "But now he is respectable. He has managed to get financial backing from men who share his ideas, and he is no longer the outlaw and raider that he once was. He has even managed to achieve some degree of protection from the law."

Grant understood that last statement to mean that bribes were involved, but bribes were not a subject that Grant liked to discuss.

"It would give me a certain amount of pleasure," he said, "to do something to hinder the work of that rascal."

"There might be an element of personal danger in the endeavor for you," Hayes said.

Personal danger was not much of a deterrent to Grant, especially when the threat came from someone like Benson, a man for whom he had little or no respect.

"I appreciate your warning," Grant said.

"If I might make a suggestion about your traveling companion," Hayes said.

"Of course."

"I believe that Sheridan would be pleased to go with you."

"Sheridan is a good man," Grant said. He did not need to add that his former lieutenant was tough as leather and thoroughly ruthless.

"Good," Hayes said. "I will see to it that arrangements are made for the trip. Would you join me for lunch?"

"No thank you," Grant said. "I must inform my family and make arrangements of my own." What he said was true, but he also knew that the White House cook was not the same man who had served under his own administration, and he did not like to trust his meals to strangers. There was always the chance that the meat would not be cooked to his taste, and he had a strong aversion to rare meat.

The truth was that Grant hated the sight of blood.

*   *   *

Colonel Benson rubbed the knobby knuckles of his wooden hand. Now that Grant's arrival in Galveston was imminent, it was time for him to begin putting his plans into action. There was much to be done, and little time to do it in.

Tollie and Patch were already at work on the docks, and although they had not yet reported to him, he assumed that they were doing as he had directed by sowing the seeds of dissent among the dockworkers. It was essential to his plans that the workers be edgy by the time Grant arrived.

Seth, on the other hand, was not working on the docks. Benson had him spending most of his time in the more disreputable parts of the city, spreading as many rumors as possible.

Since Benson did not trust Seth's mental capacities to any great extent, he had given him the easiest job. It did not really matter exactly what rumors Seth spread, as long as they were sufficiently inflammatory. Benson had given him several suggestions, and he believed that no matter how Seth garbled them, the results would still be satisfactory.

For all Benson knew, Seth might even believe the rumors were true, although Benson himself had made them all up on the spur of the moment, a fact he had neglected to mention to Seth.

The rumors included such tidbits as the notion that Norris Cuney was planning to organize the dockworkers and force out all the whites, who would then be unable to find jobs and support their wives and families.

And that Cuney had hatched a plot whereby he would become the first black governor of Texas.

And that the real purpose of Grant's trip to Galveston was for the general to give Cuney secret methods by which black militia could be trained in order for them to seize control of the city of Galveston and make it a black colony, with all whites excluded.

The fact that such rumors were ridiculous, even ludicrous, did not appear to have occurred to Seth, and Benson strongly suspected that such a thought would never occur to those people with whom Seth was likely to come into contact in the places he would be visiting. In his climb to something resembling respectability, Benson had come to have contempt for those he considered beneath him.

Benson looked around his hotel room. It was not the sort of place he would have chosen, but he did not want to reveal his presence in the city unless it became necessary.

The furniture was shabby, the curtains were tattered, the mattress was almost impossible to sleep on because he could detect on it the odor of the room's former tenants.

He was willing to suffer temporarily, however, for he believed that the results of his temporary stay in such a sty would far outweigh his present discomforts. If all worked out as he planned, it would not be Norris Cuney who occupied the governor's seat, as the rumor had it.

No, indeed.

That seat was reserved for Colonel Peter Benson, and woe be it to the man who tried to stand in his way.

Lee Strate wandered down to the whorehouse. As he got closer to the docks the smells became more numerous and strange as they all blended into one powerful odor that was different from anything Strate had experienced before.

He thought he could separate the smells associated with cattle from the rest, and maybe the smell of molasses and nuts of some kind, but these were so mingled with the scents of salt and water, decaying fish and briny ropes— among many other things—that he gave up trying to sort them out. It was impossible.

The house was very quiet when Strate approached it, as was the way with such houses at that hour of the morning. Strate supposed that the inhabitants would begin stirring about noon, perhaps later, in that they rarely got much rest until the early hours of the morning. He hoped, however, that Jack might be up and around, depending on how he had spent his evening.

The house was a two-story frame building with absolutely nothing to recommend it. It had been painted a dark green some years before, but the salt air had not been kind to it. The paint was scaling off now, revealing the boards underneath. The roof looked as if it could use repair, and the wooden blocks on which the house sat looked as if they were slowly rotting away.

Strate didn't know exactly how to approach the house. He stood there looking at it for a few minutes, and a curious passerby walked over to him.

"Better try Miss Minnie's, just up the street," the man said, his breath sour with the reminder of the previous night's whiskey. "The law here don't favor white boys goin' in a place like that."

Having offered this piece of what he no doubt considered sterling advice, the man gave Strate a friendly tap on the arm and strolled off down the street, listing just a bit to the left. As Strate watched, the man tried to compensate, but he overdid it, listing now to the right. As he made his way farther down the street, he seemd to sway from one side to the other as he made his corrections. Strate wondered if the man was just coming from an especially long night at Miss Minnie's.

He turned back to the house as the front door creaked open.

Jack was walking down the steps.

"You don't look any the worse for wear," Strate said.

"No, but you might if you keep hanging around this place," Jack said. "Let's go for a walk."

They started in the direction of the listing man.

"Some people in there were getting worried about you," Jack said.

"I didn't think anybody was awake," Strate said.

"There's *always* somebody awake in a whorehouse."

Strate thought about it and decided that Jack was probably not exaggerating. Somebody had to keep an eye on things. "I hope you were awake last night," he said.

"How do you mean that?" Jack asked.

"I mean, I hope you were trying to find out about those men who have my money."

"Our money," Jack reminded him.

"Our money, then."

"I checked, all right," Jack said. "But I didn't find out a thing. As far as I know, that man you call Tollie leads a life of purity and abstinence."

"He didn't seem like that kind to me."

"Give him a chance, then," Jack said. "He hasn't been in town but a day more than we have."

"That's right, but I've already been steered to Miss Minnie's, and I've only been out on the street for ten minutes."

"Miss Minnie's is a nice place. You might want to go there," Jack said with a straight face.

"I can't afford it."

"True, and neither can I. At least not for you. We really do need to find that money."

"I'm glad you agree. I'll start checking for Benson at the hotels. How about you?"

"I have ways to occupy my time." Jack looked back at the house.

"Oh, no," Strate said.

"It's not what you think at all. If you would like to engage in a little wager, I would bet that I find out where your men are staying before you do."

"I can't afford to bet, either."

"On the bet I would be willing to accept your marker." Strate laughed. "No thanks," he said.

Chapter Nine

Patch hated the smells of the dock. He hated the salt air and the smell of sweat and the cries of the gulls as they wheeled screeching overhead. The eye socket behind his patch stung and itched, and he felt as if there might be a small piece of grit that had somehow worked its way behind there and lodged in a fold of skin.

He wasn't fond of the work, either. Like Tollie, he was built for it, but he found no joy in trundling the huge bales from one place to another, struggling with them up the steep ramps of the ships, and finally, after compressing them further with ropes and screws, tumbling them into the hold where they would be packed as tightly as possible to make more money for some shipowner who had never been in the hold in his life and never would be. There was something about that last part that Patch found particularly galling, and it was not difficult at all for him to express outrage and indignation when he discussed things with his fellow workers.

He had to go carefully with them, however. He had to realize that whereas he had been working for only a day or so, many of them had been on the docks for years. And many of them realized that if it was not for the hard, physical labor afforded by the owners, there would be hardly any jobs at all available in Galveston for the men on the docks, men who were grateful for the money they earned and used to support themselves and their families.

So Patch had to walk a tightrope between saying what he felt about the owners on the one hand, and playing on the men's fears of losing their jobs on the other.

He began by sympathizing with the idea of a strike.

"I know I ain't been here long," he said, "but it seems to me that we work mighty hard for the money we get."

He said this to the men beside him as they strained together to get a bale up the wooden ramp of the ship they were loading. They had to get a running start with the two-wheeled hand truck they were using, with one man guiding it by the handles—Patch's job—and the men on either side of him pushing on the sides of the bale. If they lost momentum near the top, they could easily lose control of the bale and have it fall off the truck. Or, worse, have it begin rolling backward out of control.

"You're right," the man on his right said through gritted teeth. "You ain't been here long."

In fact, some of the men wondered just exactly where Patch had come from and how he had gotten his job so quickly. There was usually quite a wait for a job with the Screwmen, a wait that Benson had managed to shorten with a few well-placed bribes.

"It don't take long to see that we do a lot of sweatin', while the big bosses don't do any," Patch said. "With the money we make for them, they could afford to give us a little more of it."

They hit the top of the ramp and then had to concentrate to hold their load steady and not lose it as they steered it toward the pressing mechanism.

Patch sighed when they reached their destination. He had been standing more than he knew, and the muscles of his arms fairly quivered with the release of the tension.

Pulling the hand truck, he started back to the warehouse, the two men following along.

After they got clear of the ramp and were sure not to be overheard, Patch said, "I guess they're a-scared of the nig gers."

"Who's scared?" asked Radford, the man who had spoken before. He was short and wiry but with corded arms that looked as hard as Benson's oaken hand.

"The owners," Patch said.

"Why would they be scared of niggers?" the other man asked. A lanky, sandy-haired man, he seemed little suited to the job he was doing, but Patch could attest that he never shirked or lagged behind because there was hard work at hand.

"Because," Patch said. "You know."

"No," Radford said. "You tell us."

Patch looked around. They were passed by another three men with a bale, but no one even glanced at them. Patch wanted to give the impression that he was telling a big secret. His experience had been that the more you tried to keep things a secret, the more likely those same things were to get spread all over town in a matter of hours.

"The niggers want to take over," Patch said in a whisper.

The lanky man, whose name was Taylor, said, "I heard something about that, right enough."

"It's true," Patch assured him. "They want all the jobs on the docks for themselves. I hear that if there's a strike for fair wages, which we sure enough deserve, the niggers will move in and take over. Won't be a white man left on the docks, and won't ever be one again."

"Huh," Radford said, grunting. "They wouldn't have the gumption. We'd know how to deal with something like that."

"It wouldn't be easy to deal with 'em if the owners were behind them," Patch said. "And the people who own the docks would support the niggers. They have to keep the docks open."

"They'd be sorry if they tried that," Taylor said. His face was getting dark, or darker. It was already a deep brown from constant exposure to the sun.

"They'd try it, all right," Patch said. "You could bet on it."

"Then they'd have a helluva fight on their hands," Radford said. "Let's get to work."

They started for the warehouse again, but Patch felt a bit of satisfaction for a job well begun. If the feelings of these two men were any indication, he wasn't going to have to work too hard at getting feelings stirred up on the docks. Then, when the other part of the Colonel's plan went into effect, the part that involved the murder, things would really break loose.

Patch thought about that word—*murder*. He had killed before, but he had never thought of what he did as murder. Likely as not, whoever he killed was someone who was trying like hell to kill him. So it wasn't murder so much as self-defense.

And this wouldn't be murder, either, he told himself. It would be something else. He tried to think of the word. It had been used a lot when Booth shot Lincoln.

Assassination.

That was it, all right. Assassination. That wasn't the same as murder, was it?

Probably not, he decided, not that it made a damn bit of difference in the world to him.

He wondered how Tollie was coming along with his part of the plan. It was funny, he thought, that Tollie's being a black man didn't affect his doing the job.

And it was funny that he didn't really think of Tollie as a nigger. Tollie, after all, was his friend, someone who had ridden with him, fought beside him, slept in the same camp with him, shared his grub with him, and just generally been around him for so many years now that Patch never thought of his color or background.

To Patch, Tollie was just another man.

It was a good thing most people didn't feel that way about niggers, Patch thought. If they did, the Colonel's plan probably wouldn't stand a chance.

After he left Jack, Strate decided to walk to the beach. He would have taken one of the horse-drawn streetcars, but he didn't think he could afford it. Or Jack couldn't. Besides, he liked to walk around, get the idea of the city.

One thing he found out quickly was that Galveston was larger than he had thought. The population was over twenty-two thousand, and as he got closer to the beach, the streets got busier and busier. Surreys and riders on horseback passed him, as well as many pedestrians, the women in long, dark dresses and bonnets, the men often in business suits. He began to feel out of place in his rough Levi's, and his gun was beginning to make him feel downright uncomfortable. People who noticed it—and there were quite a few—watched him oddly as he walked past them.

That was all right, though. He was going to wear it. He was not going to take the chance of running into Patch or the others without it. They would be enough trouble even for an armed man.

As he got closer to the beach he could detect a change in the wind. Even with the houses and other buildings to serve as a break, he still had been able to tell that there was a strong onshore breeze, but now the breeze became even stronger.

There was a change in the sound of things, too. At first he thought the sound was the wind, but then he realized that he was hearing the sound of the waves washing on the beach. These were not the crashing waves he had heard in California. The sound was instead steady and somehow more leisurely, almost as if someone were breathing—in and out, in and out.

The beach was not exactly what he had expected, either. It was narrow and almost muddy. Rather than the whiteness he had expected, he saw a darker, damper sand, packed tightly together. And the water was not blue. It was more greenish, with a slightly muddy tinge where it washed up on the beach.

Despite the beach's surprising appearance, there was quite a crowd of people there, most of them in the vicinity of a huge building that a man told Strate was the Electric Pavilion. There was a bathhouse there, the man said, if Strate was of a mind to take a swim.

Strate didn't want to swim, but he did walk down the beach, which was crowded with other pedestrians, not to mention a number of carriages and horseback riders. Strate wondered who would clean up the beaches after the horses had messed it. He didn't think he would like to swim in the vicinity of one of the horses, though their riders seemed to enjoy dashing into the surf.

The Pavilion's massive front faced the Gulf of Mexico. It was lined with glass windows and doors, and there was a tower on one end. It looked like a bell tower, though the top was enclosed and Strate assumed that there was no bell inside.

Strate asked a man what the Pavilion was used for.

"Dances," the man said. "Or roller skating. That's what's on for tonight, roller skating and a greased-pig scramble. You ever seen one?"

"A roller skate?"

The man laughed. "A greased-pig scramble."

"I don't think so," Strate said.

"Well, you should be here for that. Practically everybody in town will be."

Strate thanked the man for the information and wandered on. He might give the greased-pig scramble a look. If it attracted a large crowd, maybe the men he was looking for would be there.

As he went back toward his hotel he began to look for other lodging places. There were a few near the beach, but there was no sign of Benson in any of them. One of the desk clerks told him that the fanciest hotel in town was the Tremont, down on the Strand.

The Strand was not that far from his own hotel, so Strate walked there. It was surprising to him how small the island really was. Most things were within easy walking distance.

The Strand was lined with businesses of one kind or another—cotton factories, insurance companies, banks. The hotel was not as imposing as these, but its brick front was attractive enough, and the inside had elegantly polished floors, soft chairs, and a chandelier.

Benson, however, was not there.

Strate was beginning to wonder if he had made a mistake, if he was following a false trail. After all, how did he know that Benson had really come to Galveston. There was only the word of one of Jack's cousins, who might well be wrong. Feeling low, he located a small café and had a lunch of boiled shrimp, peeling and eating them disconsolately.

Then he went back to Postoffice Street to look for Jack.

The red-light district was beginning to come to life now, in the middle of the afternoon. There was not exactly a bustle of activity, but Strate spotted young women at several windows, and the saloons and clubs were beginning to attract customers.

Jack was sitting on the steps in front of the whorehouse. He got up when he saw Strate coming and joined him in the street.

"Did you find out anything?" Jack asked.

"Not about Benson or the others," Strate said. "Did you?"

"No. I've got cousins working in most of the hotels, and I thought I would be the one to locate the Colonel or his men. Usually the people who work in hotels are the first ones to find out everything about the guests, but if any of the men we're looking for are here in Galveston, my cousins don't know about it."

"It's not as if these were ordinary-looking men," Strate said. "Patch is easy to spot, and even if I've never gotten a good look at Benson, I think I'd know him by the wooden hand."

"I don't like to suggest this," Jack said, "but do you think there is a chance that we came to the wrong place?"

Strate admitted that he had been thinking along those lines.

"On the other hand," Jack said, "they could be in hiding."

"Why?" Strate said.

"How would I know? I don't know why they came here in the first place, if indeed they did come here." Jack shook his head. "I'm beginning to regret risking my money in this venture. I should have been more like the biblical Samaritan and simply helped you out of your difficulty and left you behind.''

"I don't blame you," Strate said. "If you want to go on, I'll try to get a job here and earn some money. When I earn back what I owe you, I'll leave it with your cousin."

"But you intend to stay, no matter what?"

"That's right," Strate said. "No matter what. I think we're in the right place, and I think that they'll turn up sooner or later. This is a pretty small island. They can't hide out forever. And when they show up, I'll be ready for them. Nobody's going to shoot me, beat me, rob me, and get away with it. It's just not right."

"Five thousand dollars *is* a lot of money," Jack said.

"It's not the money," Strate said. "It stopped being the money a long time ago."

"How long ago?"

"Probably when they were kicking me."

"All right," Jack said. "I don't blame you. I can even say I understand the feeling, in a way. I'll stay. We haven't been here that long, after all. We can give it at least a few more days."

"You might never get your money back if we don't find them."

"That's right. I'm willing to take the risk. My cousins will keep looking."

"I'll keep looking, too," Strate said. He told Jack about the greased-pig scramble.

"Is there a cash prize?"

"I didn't ask."

"You might think about it. As long as you're going, anyway, we could use the money."

Strate tried to picture himself chasing a greased pig across the slick floor of the Pavilion.

"All right," he said. "I'll think about it."

Chapter Ten

Jack wasn't sure that a black man would be welcome at the greased-pig scramble. In fact, he was sure that he wouldn't, and he told Strate to go on alone. "I'll stay around here and see if your friend Tollie shows up. You never can tell who might come walking through that front door."

Strate figured that Jack knew what he was talking about. The street was getting livelier by the minute. It was just about dusk, and for every new second of darkness the noise level seemed to rise along with the number of men walking along the street looking for a good time.

The "variety shows" were getting started, and the whores were hanging out the windows of some of the houses, waving at the passersby and shouting ribald remarks.

"You're right," Strate told Jack. "If Tollie's looking for a good time, this is the place for him to come, all right."

"You sound like you might want to stay around for a while yourself," Jack said.

"Not me. This isn't my idea of fun."

"What's the matter? You don't like girls?"

"No offense to your cousin," Strate said.

"She wouldn't take any. You ought to meet her sometime."

"I'd like that, but you won't ever let me stay around long enough to meet anybody."

"I just don't want you to get in any trouble with the law."

"I don't want me to get in trouble with the law, either," Strate said. "Just tell your cousin I said howdy."

"I'll do that. Don't forget to win that money at the greased-pig scramble."

"I'll do my best," Strate said, setting off toward the beach.

The night air was cool with the Gulf breeze, and Strate enjoyed walking through the happy crowds on Postoffice Street. He wondered how much of a crowd there could be at the Electric Pavilion if there were this many people looking for entertainment of a different kind.

He soon learned that there could be a large crowd indeed. The beach was thronged with people, but there were many more women and children here than there had been on Postoffice. In fact, the only women Strate could recall seeing there had been inside the houses or saloons rather than outside.

Near the Pavilion, men and women were walking on the beach, taking the air. Children ran noisily here and there, tangling in the adults' legs and occasionally getting an ear pinched for their misbehavior. Then their yells mingled with the cries of the gulls to break the evening calm.

The Pavilion was blazing with lights, but they were gaslights. The one electric light, which was one of the main attractions, could still be viewed, but it was not the primary purpose of anyone's visit this time.

As Strate worked his way through the crowd he could hear the sound of hundreds of skates rolling over the Pavilion's hardwood floor. It was a sound that was similar in a way to the noise of the waves washing on the shore so close by, just as steady, just as prone to a rhythm of its own. Over the sound of the skates there was the faint music of a small band.

Strate lined up to pay his admission. He tried to look at it as an investment, hoping that at least one of the men he was looking for would be there, though he had to admit that it seemed more likely that they would appear on Postoffice

Street. Well, Jack had that covered, or at least part of it.

There seemed to be hundreds of people inside, and the noise of their talking, the music of the band, and the sound of the skaters all blended together into one continuous roar.

Strate didn't like it. He would much rather have been riding out on the open trail under the stars. He had never liked the feeling of being shut inside, but he liked it even less when there were this many people around him. To tell the truth, he didn't think he had ever been in a room with so many people before, even if it was such a huge place. It seemed as if the Pavilion were a block long on its longest side, though it might have been shorter. The ceiling was so high that Strate guessed it at fifteen feet and figured that he might be off by several feet, at that.

The skaters sailed around and around the center of the gigantic open space while the rest of the crowd mingled around the walls. Strate walked through the mob, trying to avoid bumping into too many of them, all the time looking for a face he recognized.

It took him quite a while to make one circuit of the room, and by the time he had done so, many more people had joined the group. He hadn't seen any of those he was looking for, but they easily could have come in during the time he was looking.

He was going to make another round, but first he stopped to watch the skaters. He had never skated himself, but he had seen it done before and liked to think that he could do it if he tried. He just couldn't think of any reason why he might try.

He liked to watch the youngsters best. They went at it with a lot of vim, moving low to the floor, waving their arms for balance, and to hell with anybody who got in their way. There were any number of collisions, several of which Strate would have bet were deliberate.

The couples were also entertaining to see, as they swayed in time to the music of the band, or tried to. It wasn't easy, what with the kids trying to skate between them or through their legs.

There were quite a few single skaters as well, and one in

particular caught Strate's eye. She looked as if she might be about twenty-one or twenty-two, and she was not dressed like most of the other young women. They were wearing proper high-necked dresses, with hems so low you could hardly see their skates. They had to skate very slowly and carefully to avoid rolling over their hems. Their hair was properly done up, and many of them were wearing hats.

Not so the woman who had caught Strate's eye. Her blond hair hung down over her high collar, and she had her skirt in her hands, hiking it up so that she could have free movement of her legs. She didn't sway slowly along in time to the music. Instead she fairly flew over the floor, giving most of the young boys a run for their money as she swung in and out, neatly avoiding any collisions with the couples among whom she dodged.

Watching her, Strate grinned. The woman clearly didn't give a damn for the social conventions. She just wanted to have a good time, and she was succeeding. There was a look of pleasure on her face, and her wide mouth was smiling. Strate liked her smile and her dark eyes and the shape that the dress did not entirely hide.

He watched her gliding along for several minutes. He didn't know how many exactly, having more or less lost track of time as he looked at her. For the first time he thought that he might enjoy being in Galveston.

But then he reminded himself that he hadn't come to the Pavilion to look at young women, no matter how pleasant that might be. He had come to look for someone quite different.

Sticking close to the wall, he began to make his way around the room again. Despite the crowd, it was not stuffy inside. The windows were open to the breeze, and he could feel it stirring on his neck as he eased along.

There was a lemonade vendor, and Strate almost bought a glass. Instead he told himself that he wasn't really thirsty. He didn't want to spend money on a cool drink when there were other things to use it for, especially when it wasn't his own money.

There was still no sign of Patch, Tollie, Seth, or Benson.

Strate was almost ready to give up, but then the band stopped playing, the skaters cleared the floor, and someone announced that the greased-pig scramble would take place shortly. There was indeed to be a cash prize of five dollars.

The rules were simple. A large wooden barrel was rolled out to the middle of the floor and set upright. To win, all you had to do was pick the pig up by the tail and put him in the barrel.

Naturally there was a catch or two.

The pig was heavily greased, which made him hard to hold, even if you could catch him, and his tail had even more grease on it than the rest of his body. Getting a grip on the tail was almost an impossibility.

And the pig had another advantage. While those who pursued him had to wear their slick-soled shoes and boots, the pig was given socks to wear, the idea being that the socks would give his hoofed feet a bitter grip on the hard-wood floor.

Strate decided to give it a try, anyway. He had already paid for his admission, which would serve as his entry fee. He didn't have anything to lose.

He pushed through the crowd to the place where the young men were gathering to take part in the scramble.

There was one person in the group he certainly had not expected to see there. Her long blond hair made her stand out from the rest, as did her dress. He could hardly believe that a woman was going to be a participant in the activity.

Neither, apparently, could a great many others Strate passed, most of them women.

"It's that Radford girl!" one matronly lady sniffed. "I do believe that she thinks she's a man."

"It's the lack of proper supervision," her companion said. "That, and her father's own wildness. What can you expect from the daughter of a dockhand?"

The young woman either did not hear such remarks or chose to disregard them. She seemed serene and undisturbed as Strate approached her.

Strate, despite the fact that he had told Jack that a whorehouse was not his idea of a good time, certainly did like women. He just didn't like whores. Even that wasn't quite the truth. He liked whores just fine; he just didn't seek them out for companionship.

The blonde was more his style. She had spirit, and she didn't seem to care what others thought about her. Besides that, she was very pretty in a natural, unaffected way.

Strate worked his way through the milling crowd until he was right beside her. Some of the other men and boys were teasing her about being in the contest.

"You ain't got a chance, Sally Radford," a boy of about twelve said. "A girl can't catch no pig!"

Sally ignored him, as she did a man of about Strate's own age who said pointedly, "If you need five dollars so bad, I can let you have it. 'Course, you might have to help me out a little, too."

Strate moved the man aside with a sharp elbow in the rib cage. The man jerked back reflexively, then got an aggressive look on his face. The look changed to one of appeasement, however, as he stared into Strate's eyes.

"Uh, excuse me," the man said, backing away.

"Watch where you're goin'," another man said as the man backed into him.

Strate wasn't looking. He had already turned his attention to the woman.

"These fellas bothering you, Miss Radford?" he said.

She looked him over calmly with her dark brown eyes. "No one is bothering me," she said. "Except possibly you. How do you know my name?"

"Someone told me," he said vaguely. "My name's Strate, Lee Strate. I surely did admire your skating."

"Thank you," she said. She had a husky voice that made Strate tingle, like a hand at the back of his neck.

"I was wondering . . ." he began.

"Then don't," she said. "The answer is no."

Strate opened his mouth to ask how she could give him an answer before he asked the question, but just then the announcer called for someone to bring in the pig.

Strate looked around and saw two men entering the Pavilion. One of them held a struggling pink pig in his arms.

The other one held a can of axle grease and a brush.

While the first man held the pig down on the floor, the second drew two pairs of socks out of his pocket and proceeded to tie them on the pig's jerking, kicking feet. It was not an easy task.

When that was accomplished, much to the pleasure of the laughing crowd, the man took the brush and stuck it deep into the grease, which he then brushed onto the pig in huge dollops, the second man slathering it around with one hand while he tried to hold the pig still with the other. He paid special attention to the tail.

While this was going on, the contestants were instructed to form a circle around the men and the pig, with the barrel in the center.

Just as the circle was complete, the pig escaped from the men, having become so slippery that they could no longer hang on to him.

Squealing in fright, the pig took off, only to be confronted by six or eight men with outstretched arms, all of whom were intent on capturing him and dropping him in the barrel that still stood in the center of the floor.

The pig's terrified squeals and the sound of his muffled hooves on the floor were soon drowned out by the laughter and yells of the crowd as they encouraged their favorites to grapple with the pig.

"Head him there, Billy! Don't let him get away!"

"Watch out, Elbert. He's comin' for you!"

"Don't move, Theron! Use your hands!"

The crowd was enjoying the spectacle much more than most of the contestants, who soon found that there was more to catching a greased pig than they had thought.

Elbert and Billy and Theron, among others, discovered that for one thing, pigs were much faster and shiftier than anticipated. They found themselves twisting hard to the left and right, and then most likely falling hard to the floor as the pig eluded them by cutting swiftly in the opposite direction.

They also found that their slippery footwear was a severe hindrance, because when they tried to cut as rapidly as the pig, their feet as often as not would go flying out from under them, causing them to land painfully on tender rumps or hips. Yelps and groans mingled with the yells of the crowd.

Strate's strategy in all of this was to wait and watch. He reasoned that sooner or later the pig would get tired, and so would most of its pursuers. He also thought that if enough of the other contestants managed to make at least some contact with the pig, some of the grease that coated it might be wiped off onto their hands and clothing, making it at least somewhat easier for a person who bided his time to get a grip.

He dashed about here and there, making a show of taking part, but being careful not to fall. His low-heeled boots put him at even more of a disadvantage than many of the others, whose shoes gave them a slight advantage in balance. A collision or two was unavoidable, but he managed not to fall too hard.

As the scrambling grew wilder, the band began to play. The additional noise seemed to stir the pig to new feats of prowess as it charged between the legs of the ones closest to it, causing several of them to perform acts worthy of a circus contortionist.

One man actually managed to get a slight grip on the pig's tail, only to find himself being pulled headfirst between his own legs. As his head went down and under, his legs flew into the air. He landed on his back with a solid thump and lay still for several seconds, all the air pushed from his lungs.

As the man was picked up and helped from the floor, Strate noticed that Sally Radford was using a strategy similar to his own. She would charge the pig, arms waving, skirts flying, but she clearly had no intention of actually trying to grab it. She was letting the others do all the work, waiting on her chance.

She looked up and saw Strate looking at her. Her level stare let him know that she recognized their similar plans.

It also told him that she intended to win.

After ten or fifteen minutes, most of the contestants were out of the game for one reason or another. Some of them were slightly injured and had been taken aside by their wives or friends to be ministered to and treated to a glass of lemonade.

Others were simply winded or tired of the chase. Several of them had long smears of grease down their shirtfronts.

The game was now left to Sally Radford, Strate, and five or six others. The pig had more room to maneuver, but the crowd had been closing in slowly, reducing the size of the circle.

Strate decided that it was time to act. He had come up with another idea. The pig's feet, encased in the socks, would be easy to grab and hold, the same socks that gave it traction on the floor giving a place to grasp it more securely.

One of the other man made a diving swipe at the pig, driving it in Strate's direction. He lowered himself to his knees to avoid falling, reached quickly out, and grabbed the two feet on the pig's left side.

The pig writhed and squealed, but Strate held on tight, lying full-length on the floor, the pig at the end of his extended arms.

The five dollars was his. All he had to do was carry the pig over to the barrel by its feet, change his grip to its tail, and let it slide into the barrel.

Nothing to it.

Then he felt something strike him sharply in the middle of his back. The sudden pain caused him to release his grip, and as he did, something soft and warm seemed to roll over his head, mashing it to the floor.

When he was able to sit up, he saw that he had lost the pig, along with the contest.

Sally Radford was carrying the squealing bundle toward the barrel, holding it exactly as Strate had planned to do, not hesitating to press it into her bosom as it kicked and struggled to get free.

When she got to the barrel, she held one foot with her left hand and grasped the tail with her right. Hoisting the pig above the opening to the barrel, she let go with her left hand. The pig was held aloft for only a second before the tail began to slip from her grip. The crowd was quiet now, and the band had stopped playing, everyone watching as the pig slid into the barrel, squealing piteously.

As it went in, Strate could hear its sock-covered hooves thudding into the side of the barrel.

For a moment Strate was angry at the way he had been beaten—and by a woman, at that. Then he grinned. What the hell. It was a good trick, and he only wished that he had thought of it himself.

Still, he could have used that five dollars.

Chapter Eleven

Even a whorehouse has a kitchen, and that was where Jack had spent most of his time. His cousin didn't want him mingling too much with her girls, which was all right with Jack, as long as he could get information from them in case they encountered anyone named Tollie.

He was talking with the cook, a fat woman named Annie, telling her about his mule, William, and listening to the noise from outside as it came through the wide-open windows of the kitchen.

"He's a hammerheaded devil, and I hated to leave him there in Houston," Jack said. "I know he's being well taken care of, but I like to do for him myself."

Annie understood perfectly. "I'd sure hate to be parted from my little dog," she said. "That little dog knows just what I'm thinkin' most of the time, and sometimes I think he even tries to talk to me."

They were sitting at the kitchen table, which was covered with a coarse white cloth that had been drawn tight and tacked down under the edges. Whenever anyone ate, Annie scraped the crumbs off the cloth with a wooden scraper. Most of the girls ate a hearty breakfast when they got up at around two or three in the afternoon, and didn't eat again until just before they went to sleep in the early-morning hours. Annie had cooked supper for Jack, however, and he had just finished a platter of fried fish and hush puppies.

He started to tell her that he sometimes believed that he and William could communicate when there was a burst of sound from somewhere down the block.

"I 'spect that's from that variety show," Annie said. "They got them a woman there, Miss Tessie, that th'ows the Indian clubs. They say it's quite a sight to see."

"People pay money to see somebody throw Indian clubs?" Jack said. "I don't understand why. That's not much of an accomplishment."

"Honey, it ain't what she does, it's how she does it." Annie laughed. "And I 'spect that what she wears while she does it has somethin' to do with it too."

"I thought it was probably something like that," Jack said, though he hadn't actually thought of it. Galveston's variety shows were something new to him.

"Listen," Annie said, "the things goin' on in those shows is a sight. They got women pullin' the handles on the beer kegs in those halls, for one thing, and they got dancers that don't wear no more than a by-god."

Jack wasn't sure what a by-god wore, but he got the idea.

"Wouldn't catch me in a place like that," Annie said.

Jack didn't ask her why she was willing to cook in a whorehouse but wouldn't go to a variety show. He was sure there was a good reason, but he would have bet it wasn't a logical one, and he didn't want to get into an argument with Annie. He liked her.

He was about to change the subject back to William when his cousin came in. Her name was Lavinia. She was a tall woman, almost as tall as Jack, and very thin. If she had been a man, she and Annie could have posed for the pictures of Jack Spratt and his wife that Jack had seen in the nursery-rhyme book he had learned to read from so many years ago. She had on a shimmery orange dress that didn't cover her ankles, and there was a feather boa wrapped around her neck. Jack had no idea how old she was. She might have been thirty or sixty. There was just no way to tell by looking.

"What's this about a man named Tollie?" she said. She

had a raspy, smoky voice, and Jack had heard that she once had been a singer.

"I'm looking for him," Jack said. "He owes me some money." That might not have been exactly true, but it was close enough. "Is he here?"

"He might be," Lavinia said. She described a man who sounded pretty much like the one Lee had described to Jack.

"That sounds like him, all right," Jack said. "Where is he?"

"He is occupied. I don't want you to bother him while he is with one of my girls, or even while he is in my house. I don't want any trouble here."

Jack could understand that. Galveston was obviously a wide-open town, but even in a place like that, there were proprieties that had to be observed in order for business to go on as usual. There was the laws to think of, naturally, and of course an unhappy customer was not likely to provide any return business.

"We can't even be sure that he is the man you're looking for," Lavinia went on. "We don't want to make any mistakes of identity if we can avoid them, so Sylvie is going to try to find out his name."

Jack assumed that Sylvie was the girl Tollie—or whoever it was—was visiting. "That's fine," he said.

"If it does indeed prove that the man is the one you are looking for, Sylvie will let us know as he leaves. Then you can follow him and do whatever it is that you feel necessary. All I ask is that you wait until he is at least a block from this house before you do it."

"I don't really think I'll do anything," Jack said. "If he's my man, I'll just follow him to wherever it is he's staying. I'm interested in his friends, too."

"Good," Lavinia said. "You just wait here in the kitchen and I will let you know later about the man. I think you can count on Sylvie to find out what you want to know. Sylvie is very good at things like that."

She gave her boa a toss and left the kitchen.

"She right about that Sylvie," Annie said. "That Sylvie

do it just like a snake, so they tell me. Best girl in the house, and a hard worker, too.''

Jack had seen Sylvie, and he suspected that Lavinia was right. Annie, too, probably, but it wasn't something he wanted to talk about. He started telling Annie about William again.

The crowd wasn't particularly pleased with Sally Radford's victory. There was a smattering of applause, nothing more, and even though Strate was a stranger, a number of people came up to him and told him that they thought he had been cheated of his prize.

"You had that pig fair and square," one man said, laying his hand on Lee's shoulder. "It was me, I'd have a word with the headman about that Radford girl."

Strate shrugged off the man's hand. "She won," he said. "No need to make trouble."

The man looked at Strate as if Strate had lost his mind, then walked off into the crowd, shaking his head and mumbling about five dollars being a lot of money. He was right, but when you'd already lost a thousand times that much just recently, five dollars sort of lost its importance.

Strate decided to head on back to his hotel. It was getting late, and he hadn't spotted anyone he wanted to see in the crowd.

He was almost out the door when Sally Radford caught up with him.

"I'd like to buy you a glass of lemonade," she said. Her hair was in disarray and there was a smear of axle grease on her right cheek, but she was still one of the best-looking women Strate had seen in a long time.

"All right," he said.

She went over to the vendor and bought the lemonade. "Let's take this outside," she suggested.

They went outside and stood on the porch. There were quite a few people taking the air. Even though the Pavilion was well ventilated, the huge crowd, combined with all the activity, had made it a bit stuffy inside.

Now and then breezes pushed the clouds aside and allowed the stars and the moon to peek through. The wind stirred Sally Radford's hair as she took a sip of her drink.

"I'm sorry about what I did," she said.

"That's all right," Strate told her. "I didn't mind."

She laughed. "You minded."

Strate grinned. "Well, maybe a little."

"I had to win," Sally said, all the laughter suddenly gone from her voice. "I had to show them."

"Show who?"

She looked back inside. "All of them. Every one of them."

Strate drank the lemonade. It was sweet and tart at the same time. He didn't ask why.

"They think they're so smart," Sally said. "They think they know the right way and the wrong way, and they think everybody should behave the way they do."

Strate still didn't say anything.

"You want to go for a swim?" Sally asked.

Strate had never been swimming in the surf. "I'm not dressed for it," he said.

"You don't dress for it at all," Sally said. "That's the point."

Strate swallowed hard, his mouth suddenly dry even though he had just been drinking lemonade.

"I'm not sure what you mean," he said.

"We go in without our clothes on," she said. She seemed exasperated at his inability to comprehend.

"Is that, uh, legal?"

Sally stomped her foot on the wooden decking of the porch. "Of course it's not. That's the point."

"It is?"

"Oh, don't be such an old fogy. Of course it is. Why do it if it's something that everyone else does."

"You mean, nobody's ever done it?"

"You sound like a newcomer. Of course people have done it. A whole crowd of men and women got arrested about a year ago for nude bathing right along this very beach. It scandalized half the town."

Strate was beginning to realize, if he hadn't already, that he was in the company of a quite unconventional young woman, one who not only didn't care what others thought of her but who also went out of her way to create what most people would have regarded as an unfavorable impression.

He found himself in an interesting situation. He hadn't come to the Pavilion to meet a woman, but now that he had, he thought he might as well make the most of it.

"I'll go swimming with you," he said. "You want to go right here, in front of everybody?"

"Not here. But only a little way down the beach. We don't have to be in sight of everyone. I don't want to do this just to be arrested."

Strate was tempted to ask her just exactly why she did want to go swimming, but he didn't. He put his glass down on the railing and followed her out onto the beach.

He did not notice the man who was watching them, a mush-mouthed man who had come to the Pavilion only a short time before because he thought it would be a good place to tell people about how Grant was coming to Galveston to start the war all over again.

As soon as she was off the porch, Sally took off her shoes and ran down to the surf. She walked along at the edge of the water, letting it swirl in around her ankles. Strate left his boots on and stayed clear of the water. Only this far from the Pavilion, the sound of the wind and the waves easily drowned out the sounds of the crowd and the music of the band.

They walked for what Strate judged to be a half mile. He could still see the Pavilion in the distance, its lights flickering like tiny beacons.

"This is far enough," Sally said, stopping and looking at Strate. He could see her clearly, even though the clouds were still thick. Somehow they seemed only to diffuse the light of the nearly full moon so that he could almost see the color of her eyes.

She walked out of the water and past Strate. "I'm going to put my clothes back up here," she said. "I don't want to get them wet."

Strate followed her. "That sounds like a good idea," he said.

With their backs to each other, they got out of their clothes. Strate was in no hurry, and Sally finished before he did. She ran down to the water without a word.

Strate followed quickly. He watched as her white body entered the surf, the splashes catching the light as she kicked her way out into the deeper water. When the water reached her calves, she plunged headfirst into the small waves.

Strate hit the water expecting it to be cold, but it was not. In fact, it was quite warm, warmer than the night air, though he knew that he would be very cold when he got out and the wind hit him.

The bottom felt solid, almost like the sand across which he had run, and the waves didn't bother him. He had learned to swim in a farm pond with a muddy bottom, and he figured that this couldn't be much different, just a lot bigger. He had never worn anything when he went swimming there, either, but he had to admit that the only ones around were his brothers.

When he got out far enough, he ducked under the water.

That was when he got his first real surprise.

The water got into his eyes and his nose, stinging his eyes and running back into his throat.

It was like swallowing a handful of raw salt.

He stood up, pawing at his hair to get it off his face, rubbing at his eyes and coughing and choking so that he was bent over.

When he had coughed up most of the ocean, or so he felt, he heard someone laughing.

"You're a newcomer, all right," Sally said. "I bet you've never been in the surf before."

He could see only her head sticking out of the water. It was as if she were sitting on the bottom, which he decided she probably was. Her head bobbed gently up and down with the motion of the waves, and for the first time he noticed a gentle pulling around his ankles, as if a careful hand were urging him to swim out farther or playfully trying to coax him to dive under.

Shaking his head once more, he jumped for Sally. If he was going to feel foolish, he was not going to be alone. He intended to push her head under and see how she liked it.

But going under didn't bother Sally. She ducked under herself, easily eluding him.

He stood looking for her, seeing only the waves, tipped with foam and light.

Then a very real and not so gentle hand grabbed his ankle and jerked, hard. He fell, going down and under, getting another nose and mouthful of the salty water.

This time he came up sputtering, but at least he wasn't coughing and choking.

He looked around for Sally, who poked her head out of the water and then ducked right back under.

He jumped for her again, this time getting a hand on her leg. He was not able to get a good grip, however. She was almost as slick as the greased pig had been.

They both came up laughing.

They looked at each other and the laughing stopped.

Strate moved toward her.

This time she didn't move away.

He took her in his arms and pulled her to him. The cold tips of her breasts pushed into his chest, and they kissed. Her lips were cold, too.

When they broke apart, Strate felt light-headed and happy. He had never felt exactly like that before.

He was about to kiss her again when he heard the gunshots, and the first bullet smacked into the water beside them.

Chapter Twelve

Tollie, Jack decided, was much of a man. He was upstairs with Sylvie for considerably longer than the usual time for such transactions; so much longer, in fact, that Jack began to worry about whether the man was ever coming down. And besides being much of a man, Tollie must have had a sizable bankroll. Lavinia's girls were not the type to let a man linger unless he could afford to pay for his pleasure, and pay well.

When Tollie finally came down, Lavinia came to the kitchen door and tipped Jack a nod, as if to say, "He's your man."

Jack slipped out the back door, high-stepped to the front of the house, and watched Tollie walking away. It was so late that the crowds had thinned out in the street, so Jack let Tollie get about a block away before stepping into the street to follow him.

Something went wrong.

Jack was never sure what gave him away. Maybe he had followed a little too closely, or maybe Tollie was just a man so used to being hunted that his instincts warned him immediately when someone was on his trail.

For whatever reason, Tollie knew that he was being followed.

Jack didn't catch on right away. When Tollie turned down

an alleyway between a saloon and another cathouse, Jack didn't think anything of it. Tollie could have been taking a shortcut, or he might have been staying in a house in the neighborhood. Jack was hardly even suspicious.

When he turned into the alley, Tollie had disappeared.

Jack realized then that the big man had been aware of someone behind him. He ran down the alley, not worrying about the noise he was making, hoping that he could catch up.

He didn't.

He came to an intersecting alley and didn't know whether to turn left, right, or keep going straight ahead.

He heard a loud noise to his left and looked in that direction, suddenly noticing a terrible stench in the air, a stench quite different from anything he had noticed in the city so far. A man began yelling and cursing at the top of his lungs.

It was the night-soil collector. Galveston did not yet have a sewer system, and the human wastes that were deposited in the privies were placed in barrels and picked up in carts late at night. Tollie had run into the carter, knocking him down and turning over the barrel of excrement.

The carter's language was appropriate to his trade, at least in its filthiness, but Jack was thankful for the alarm. He ran in that direction.

Others, not so happy to be disturbed, leaned out their windows and shouted for the carter to shut his mouth so that they could sleep. The offended man, however, did not get quiet. If anything, his curses increased in volume and intensity.

Jack passed him by, trying not to think of where he was stepping as his feet slopped in the slimy substance that had spilled from the overturned barrel. If Tollie had gotten any of the foul mess on himself, he would be easy to track. In fact, now that Jack realized what was back in the alleys, he found that the smell filled his nose and permeated the entire atmosphere. Or maybe he only smelled himself. It was hard to tell.

Jack would have thought that Tollie would be tired after

his exertions with Sylvie, but instead the man seemed to have been charged with energy. Jack could not gain on him.

Finally, after they had run for at least five blocks, Tollie began to slow. Then he stopped.

Jack ran faster. He was sure that he had his man now, and he could almost feel that five thousand dollars being counted out into his hand, or at least half of it.

But Tollie hadn't stopped to give Jack the money.

He turned, and fire seemed to leap from his hand.

Jack heard the explosion of the pistol shot, and when he thought about it later, he was convinced that he'd heard the bullet whiz by his head. He never told anyone that part of it, however. He was afraid they would think he was lying.

There was nowhere to hide except behind a barrel of night soil, but Jack didn't hesitate. He ducked down behind the barrel.

The second bullet hit the barrel dead on, shaking it but not dislodging the cover. Jack could hear something glopping out the small hole on the opposite side of the barrel.

How had he gotten into this mess? He didn't have a pistol, never had owned one. Never had needed one, for that matter, not until he got hooked up with Lee Strate. Not for the first time, he wished he had gone on to San Antonio.

Tollie fired again.

The barrel shuddered again. Tollie had hit the same stave, which cracked under the strain. More of the contents spilled out.

Jack could hardly breathe.

Tollie was running again. Jack heard his retreating footsteps, along with the yells from several houses, all of them saying something about calling for the police.

Jack thought it was time to get out of there. He obviously wasn't going to catch up with Tollie, and he wasn't even sure he wanted to.

He just hoped he could get back to his cousin's house before someone tried to dump him in the Gulf with the rest of the droppings.

* * *

Strate couldn't believe he was in the middle of the ocean, naked, without his gun.

And someone was shooting at him.

It really wouldn't have mattered where he was, however. He had not worn his gun to the Pavilion. He had not thought that anyone would make a try for him there, and he had thought that a greased-pig scramble was no place for an armed man.

Now he realized how wrong he had been, and he wondered if in some way Sally was involved in what was happening.

He stopped wondering when she screamed and tried to bury herself in the water. She was too scared to be a part of the shooting.

She might have been scared, but she was smart. The best place to be when bullets were flying at you was underwater, and when the second shot rang out, Strate ducked under with her.

He knew that the whiteness of their bodies made them vivid targets if they stood up, but his own red hair would not show up as well if only his head were above water. Fortunately the water had darkened Sally's blondness, so that she could come up for a breath without too much danger.

He poked his head through the surface and looked around.

He saw the muzzle flash from the beach, but the bullet splatted the water several yards off to the right. There was no way he could get to the beach without being seen and locate whoever was shooting, but at least they would probably be safe from him.

When Sally's head came up, Strate whispered, "It's all right. He can't see us."

"Are you sure?" Sally's voice had a distant quaver in it. Strate might not have been used to swimming in the surf, but she was equally unused to being shot at.

"Pretty sure. He's shooting off to the right. Let's drift a little to the left."

They did, drifting easily, always aware of that gentle but persistent tugging around their feet.

There were two more shots, which went even farther to their right, and then a long silence.

"What if he finds our clothes?" Sally said. She was getting her spunk back quickly.

Strate hadn't thought about it. There wasn't much that he had to lose, but he didn't relish the thought of having to make his way back to the hotel buck-naked. He tried to think what Sally would feel if she had to get home that way.

"We'll just have to take the chance," he said. There was no way he would get out of the water too quickly.

"Maybe if we went down more to the left, you could get out of the water and sneak back on him," Sally said.

Strate looked at her pale face. Why hadn't he thought of that? Probably because he didn't like the thought of sneaking up on an armed man with nothing to protect himself except his bare hands. And bare other things.

But it seemed like their best chance, so he let himself drift farther to the left. When he thought he was about the right distance away to sneak out of the water unseen, he told Sally that he was going ashore.

"Be careful," she said.

He told her that he intended to be. He eased along, letting the waves carry him to shore. He went the last few yards on his belly, trying to stay beneath the water as long as possible. When he was scraping along on the sand, he got up into a crouch and ran up on the beach.

He felt ridiculous, running along like a duck without a stitch of clothing on. His eyes searched the dark for whoever had been shooting at them, but he could see nothing.

There was almost no place that anyone could hide on the beach. There were no dunes to speak of, and the beach was flat and level. Once he thought he saw movement and flattened himself on the sand, but there was no one there.

Eventually he had gotten at least as far as the spot where he had originally entered the water. He had seen nothing and no one. The beach was as deserted as the Kansas prairie. There was no life there except the few plants that waved in the sea breeze.

He searched the area carefully for several minutes but

found nothing to indicate that anyone had been there. There were probably footprints in the sand, but he couldn't see them in the dim light.

It was then that he realized he didn't know where he had left his clothes. There was no way to tell whether they had been stolen or whether he simply didn't know where to locate them.

He went back down the beach to find Sally.

He wouldn't have been able to find her, either, if she hadn't called his name from the water.

"You can come out now," he said. "It's safe."

"What about my clothes?"

"I can't find them," he admitted.

"Were they stolen?"

"I don't know. I just can't find them."

"Damn."

Strate wasn't sure he had ever heard a woman curse before, at least not a respectable one, but he knew how she felt. He felt the same way. He didn't know what to do with his hands, whether to try to cover himself or to act as if nothing unusual were going on. When they had been in the water together, being naked had seemed like the most natural thing in the world. Now it seemed faintly absurd, as if they were acting in some saloon farce.

"I'm going to swim back down to where we got in," she said. "You meet me there."

Strate started walking back down the beach, trying to keep her in sight, but it was too dark. He finally stopped and waited for her to get out of the water.

When she did, she was fifty yards away, farther down the beach than Strate had gone. He hadn't thought they had drifted that far.

"You stay there," she yelled. "I'll find the clothes, if they're here."

He watched her pale form move along the beach, bent in search of the clothes. After a minute she picked up something.

"Here they are," she called.

He waited until she had dressed, then walked toward her.

She moved away from his clothes, her back to him. He pulled on his clothing glumly. It was strange how things could change so quickly, all because of a few gunshots.

"I'm sorry," she said.

Strate was sorry, too, but he didn't want to make a big thing of it. "Don't worry," he said. "Probably just someone who was disappointed about not winning the pig scramble."

"I don't think so," she said. "This isn't the kind of town where people carry guns and go around shooting them."

Strate hadn't realy thought that it was. He had been pretty sure all along that the shots had been intended for him. And if they had been, then it was almost a certainty that Patch and the boys were in town and that one of them had seen him at the Pavilion. He wondered which one it was.

He got his clothing adjusted and went to stand beside Sally. Her hair was tangled and matted by the salt water, but she still looked very pretty to Strate. If he had been angry with Patch before, because of the money, he was even angrier now. It was one thing to lose five thousand dollars. It was another thing to lose his chance with Sally Radford. He wondered which loss meant the most to him.

They began walking back in the direction of the Pavilion.

"I really shouldn't be going swimming with strange men," Sally said. "My father wouldn't like it if he knew. Especially the part about being shot at."

"I wouldn't blame him," Strate said. "I don't like it much myself."

"Does it happen often?"

"No," Strate said. "Not often."

"Just so that we're not such strangers, why don't you tell me a little about yourself," Sally said. "Who knows? We may see each other again."

"I hope so," Strate said.

They walked along in silence for several yards.

"Well?" Sally said.

Strate sighed. There was no reason not to tell her. "I came here looking for some men," he said. "They took something of mine."

"You think they're the ones who shot at us?"

"Probably. They don't like me much."

"Why not?"

"I don't know. I never did anything to them. I guess there are just people like that. They take a dislike for someone, and they can't let go of it."

"What did they take from you?"

"Money," Strate said.

"It must have been a lot of money."

Strate told her how much.

"That's a lot, all right."

"A friend is helping me get it back. He's staying at a house on Postoffice Street."

Sally looked at him.

"It's his cousin's house."

"Oh. Why wasn't he at the Pavilion tonight?"

"He's a black man," Strate said.

"Oh," she said again. "These men you're looking for. What are they doing in Galveston?"

"I don't know," Strate said. "They work for a man called Colonel Benson. I think they came here with him.

"But you don't know why?"

"No."

"What do they look like?"

Strate didn't think it was very likely that she had seen any of them, but he described them as best he could.

"The one with the patch," Sally said. "My father knows a man like that."

"He does?"

"He works on the docks," Sally said. "He just started yesterday."

"Well, I'll be damned," Strate said.

Chapter Thirteen

Annie wouldn't let Jack come back in, not even at the back door."

"Not until you clean yourself up," she said. "You smell just like you fell in one of them privy barrels." She held her nose with her thumb and first finger. "Whoooeeee. You stink somethin' awful."

Jack had to admit that she was right, but he didn't know what to do about it.

"You take ever' single stitch off you," Annie said. "Then you go over to the rain barrel and wash off. You let me get you some soap."

He waited for a minute, standing by the back steps.

Annie returned to the door with a bar of hard soap and tossed it out to him. "You scrub all over with this. Then maybe I'll let you in the house."

The rain barrel was nearly full, and Jack suspected that there was no shortage of clean water to fill it, considering the climate of the coastal towns. He threw his clothes in a pile on the ground, splashed water all over himself, and scrubbed off with the soap. He scrubbed hard and long, trying to rid himself of the stench.

When he was through, he left his clothes where they were and went back to the kitchen door. Annie had laid a shirt and a pair of pants on the small back porch.

He put on the clothes. They didn't fit particularly well, and he wondered where they had come from. He had another shirt and pair of pants in his room, but these obviously had not come from there.

He went into the kitchen. Annie was sitting at the table.

"I sure don't see how anybody could come home smellin' like that," she said. "Where you been?"

He told her.

"I thought you smelled that way. I sure didn't think you'd really done it," she said.

"I didn't fall in the barrel. It just splashed on me."

"Same thing."

"I guess you're right." He didn't see any use in arguing.

"You didn't get to talk to that man, then."

He agreed that he hadn't talked to anyone.

"Oughta talk to that Sylvie, then. Maybe she found out somethin' about him. Where he live or somethin'."

"I'll talk to her later. I expect she's still working."

"Probably is. You want me to fry you up some more fish while you waitin'?"

It occurred to Jack that eating wasn't a bad idea. Chasing men through alleys was a good way to work up an appetite.

"Thanks," he said. "That sounds good."

Soon the kitchen was filled with the odor of battered fish being fried in sizzling oil. Even the Gulf breeze couldn't entirely blow the smell away. That was fine with Jack. The smell was making his mouth water.

After he ate his second supper Jack had to wait another two hours before Sylvie was through for the evening. Or the morning. It was nearly five A.M., and Jack was getting sleepy.

"That Sylvie is a right lively girl," Annie told him. "Seems she has a lot of men that ask for her special. I don't know what it is that she got, but she got plenty of it."

Lavinia had come in to hear the story of what had happened with Tollie, and she took Jack up to Sylvie's room. "She's a smart girl," Lavinia said. "But I don't know what that man might have told her. I don't like for my girls to go questioning their customers. Don't expect too much."

Jack didn't expect anything. The way his luck was running so far, he'd be lucky if Sylvie even remembered Tollie.

She did, however. She was small and coffee-colored, and she especially remembered how big Tollie was and how deep his voice was.

"He was hard to satisfy, though," she said. "I had to charge him double, 'cause of how long he stayed. But he said he didn't care. Said he had plenty of money to spend." She shook her head. "Didn't show me none of it, though. Just paid what he owed and left."

My money, Jack thought. *The bastard is spending my money to have a good time with these girls.*

"Did he say anything about where he was staying or what he was doing here in town?" Jack asked.

"Not a word," Sylvie said. "And I didn't ask him, either. Miss Lavinia didn't say anything about that."

"That's all right," Jack said. "I was just wondering."

He went downstairs to the little room beside the kitchen where he was staying. A number of the girls were eating breakfast—or supper rather. For them it was the end of the day, not the beginning. They all greeted Jack cheerily, but he didn't linger to talk to them. In the first place his cousin wouldn't have approved. In the second place he was dog-tired. He closed his door, lay down on the cot that was crammed in there, and was asleep in only a minute or two, the sound of the women's voices falling on his ears like the sound of the surf.

Strate had gotten back to his hotel much earlier, and he fell asleep thinking about what Sally Radford had told him about the man called Patch.

"My father says he came to work yesterday," Sally said. "Everyone thought it was funny that a man none of them had ever seen before could just come down to the docks and start right to work. Those jobs aren't easy to get as a rule, and that's why my father mentioned it to me."

"I don't suppose he knows where Patch is staying or anything," Strate said.

"I doubt it. He did say that the man was a troublemaker. All he talks about is the trouble between the dockworkers and the people who own the docks. And about the Screwmen and the Cotton Jammers."

"Who?"

Sally explained to him about the two organizations that loaded the cotton onto the ships, and she told him that the Screwmen were considering a strike.

"Some of them are worried about what might happen if they strike," she said. "They're afraid the black workers will try to take over the docks and freeze out the whites."

Strate couldn't figure out why Patch would be working on the docks in the first place, what with a third of Strate's money in his pockets, and he couldn't see any reason why Patch would be stirring up trouble.

"Do you think I could talk to your father?" he asked.

"Not tonight," Sally said. "It's too late, and we aren't really dressed appropriately."

She laughed, and Strate had to laugh with her. They were both bedraggled-looking, having put on their clothes still wet from their swim. At least the walk back to the Pavilion had warmed them up. The cool wind and the wet clothes had been very uncomfortable for a while.

"I'll walk you home, then," he said, and she agreed. She lived on Avenue O, not too far from the Pavilion.

The frame house was dark when they arrived. "My father doesn't wait up on me," she said. "Why don't you come by tomorrow afternoon after he gets back from his job. You could talk to him then."

Strate had something else in mind, but he said, "I'll try. If I'm not here, don't mention it." He paused. "I would like to see you again."

She leaned toward him and kissed him lightly on the lips, then ran up the steps. "I'll be here tomorrow, too," she said. Then she went inside.

As he lay in the bed looking at the pressed-tin ceiling of his room, Strate remembered the pressure of her lips, and that memory almost blotted out his thoughts about Patch and what he was doing on the Galveston docks.

He dragged his mind back to its original train of thought. Benson must have had a reason for going to Galveston and disappearing, just as Patch must have a reason for working where he was. None of that really mattered, however. What mattered was the money.

And, of course, getting shot at.

Now that he was certain that Patch was in town, Strate didn't find getting shot at so surprising. He could think of at least three people who were probably in Galveston and who had reason for wanting him out of the way. It wasn't that he was any threat to them, he thought. It was just that he was an inconvenience.

He wondered which one of them had spotted him. Now that they knew he was around, they would be watching for him. He would have to be careful, more careful than he had been so far. He could tell Jack the next day that they were on the right track.

He fell asleep wondering why whoever had shot at him hadn't stayed around to finish the job.

Seth was trying to explain the same thing to Patch.

"I think maybe I got him," he said, "but it's hard to say for sure." His heavy drawl made the last two words sound like *foah shoah*.

"You should have stayed around to see," Patch said.

"I was afraid somebody would hear the shots. You can't ever tell who else might take a notion to go for a swim."

"I can't believe that bastard has followed us down here from Houston," Patch said. "How could he know we were going to be here, anyway?"

"I don't know," Seth said.

"The Colonel won't be happy about this, that's for sure," Patch said.

"Uh, maybe we don't have to tell him," Seth said. "We didn't ever tell him the fella was in Houston, did we?"

The answer to that question was no. Patch hadn't seen any reason to tell Benson about the man they'd robbed, or the money they'd taken. It didn't have anything to do with the job they were on, and Benson might have thought it would be a distraction.

Well, Patch thought, he would have been right. It was a distraction, all right. But there was no way they could have known that it would have been. Who would have expected that cowboy to turn up in Houston, much less in Galveston?

"Wait a minute," he said. "What if he was just here by accident? What if he didn't know we were here?"

"Huh?" Seth said.

"What if he was just here for his health, or to go for a naked swim with a pretty girl? He might not even have known we were around. But you can damn well bet he knows it now."

"Huh?"

There were times when Patch got impatient with Seth, and this was one of them. He just didn't seem to catch on to things.

"You should either have killed him for sure, or left him alone," Patch said. "If you didn't kill him, he knows that somebody's after him."

Seth finally caught on. "You mean, he might catch on . . . catch on . . . that . . . that . . ." He was too excited to get it out.

"Damn right," Patch said, not waiting for Seth to finish. "He might catch on that we're here, and he might just interfere with what the Colonel wants us to do."

"So we better . . . better . . ."

"We better tell the Colonel," Patch said. But he really didn't want to do it.

Patch started to get dressed. He and Seth were staying in a boardinghouse near the docks, but neither of them was interested in the pleasures offered by Postoffice Street and the nearby areas. Seth had his rumors to spread, and Patch was too tired after his day's work to have any energy left over for women. He had come home right after finishing up and gone to bed right after eating supper. Seth had waked him up to tell him about spotting the redhaired man they had robbed.

"The Colonel won't like us getting him up at this time of

night," Patch said, wondering just what time it was, exactly.

"We gotta tell him, though," Seth said, back under control again.

"I know it, dammit," Patch said, pulling on his heavy work shoes. "I just hate to have to do it."

"Should we go get Tollie?"

Patch thought about it. "No," he said. "I can tell him tomorrow."

Colonel Benson sat up in the bed, his back braced by two of the inadequately stuffed feather pillows provided by his cheap hotel. The light was provided by a coal-oil lamp, since the hotel did not have gaslight, and there were wavering shadows all around the room.

"Let me get this straight," Benson said. "You robbed a man on the way to Houston, despite the fact that you knew I had a job for you."

"I know we shouldn't've done it," Patch said apologetically. "We just couldn't resist it. He was just such easy pickings."

"I hope your efforts were adequately rewarded," Benson said with a touch of sarcasm.

"Yessir, they were," Patch said. "We got five thousand dollars."

Benson was impressed in spite of himself. "Where would a man on the trail get that kind of money?"

"We didn't think to ask him," Patch said.

"Nevertheless, you've put our mission in danger," Benson said.

"We never meant to do that," Patch said. "We didn't even know what you wanted us to do down here."

Benson looked significantly at Seth, and Patch realized that one of them still didn't know the whole story.

"I don't think he'll interfere," Patch said, not being entirely truthful. "We just thought you ought to know about him."

"He can interfere without intending it. This is a very sensitive mission," Benson said.

"Maybe Seth killed him," Patch said, though he was not

really hopeful that the man was dead. Seth was not exactly a sure shot.

"And maybe the South won the war," Benson said. "We cannot afford to take the chance. I want this man put out of the way."

"That might not be so easy," Patch said. "We don't know where to find him."

"I want him found," Benson said. "I want him put out of the way."

Patch shook his head. "I'm doing just about all I can down there on the docks. I don't have time to go hunting anybody." He was hoping that the Colonel would tell him to give up his job and look for the redhead. He didn't think he could find him, but the search would be better than working on the ships.

"Seth will have to find him, then."

Both men looked at Seth, who had not said a word since he entered the room.

Realizing that they were talking about him, Seth jerked his head around and looked at them. He had been staring at something else.

"Huh?" he said.

"I want you to find that man again," Benson said. "Then I want you to tell Patch where he is."

"I don't know if I can find him," Seth said.

"You have two days," Benson said. "I want him by then."

"But I don't know—"

"Find him," Benson said. There was a note of finality in his voice that said any further argument was useless.

Seth turned away, saying nothing.

"Wait outside, Seth," Benson said.

Seth got up and went out of the room, closing the door behind him.

"Grant will be here in two days," Benson said when Seth was gone.

"That doesn't give us much time to talk things up," Patch said. "I don't think we can do a lot of good in two more days."

"It's not just what you can say in two days. It's what the men are already thinking and feeling, in combination with what you can say. Two days is plenty of time to play on the discontent and dissatisfaction that already exist."

"I just don't see what good all this will do," Patch said.

"Grant was the architect of the downfall of the South," Benson said. "He was, and is, a symbol of everything I fought against. We have a chance here to do more mischief in one day than has been done to the North since the war, and I intend to grasp the opportunity while it exists."

Benson sat up a little straighter against the pillows. "If we can set the white man against the black, we can begin a revolution that will accomplish what the war should have. We can push the black race into the subjugation that is its natural condition. Failing that, we can rid the state of Texas of a malign force for evil at the very least."

Patch nodded. He never really understood the Colonel when he started talking like that. He didn't think even the Colonel really believed that a man like Tollie should be subjugated, or even that he could be. But the Colonel had always been a little cracked on the subject of black men.

"You understand what I am saying, don't you?" Benson said. "We can't fail in what we set out to do here."

That much Patch could understand.

When he got outside, Patch saw Seth standing in the shadows at the corner of the building. He walked over and grabbed him by the arm.

"What the hell were you staring at in there?" he said. "You looked like some kind of idiot."

"It was the hand," Seth said. "Didn't you see the hand?"

"The hand? I didn't see any hand."

"It was there," Seth said. "It was right there by the bed."

He could still see it in his mind's eye, the oaken hand, sitting there on a little table by the Colonel's bed. It was not clenched, but its fingers were slightly curved, as if it were grasping something. Seth wondered what it was supposed to be holding.

"Come on," Patch said. "It's time for me to get some more sleep."

He gave a tug on Seth's arm, and they walked off down the street toward the boardinghouse.

Once Seth looked back over his shoulder. Patch didn't ask what he'd seen.

Chapter Fourteen

Strate was up early the next morning, but though he stood in front of the whorehouse for a long time, Jack never came out. Wondering what might be the matter but not wanting to go up to the door and ask, for fear that he might get in serious trouble, Strate went to eat breakfast.

After he ate, he bought a newspaper and read it while standing on the corner and waiting for Jack to put in an appearance. He found out that General Grant was expected to be in town in two days and that there would be a gala reception and ball at the Electric Pavilion, "to welcome our distinguished guest to our fair city." The article also informed Strate that somewhere in the neighborhood of five thousand people were expected to attend the ball.

Strate could believe it. The Pavilion would hold that many people and probably have room to spare. He wondered if Sally Radford would be going, and then he thought about what it would be like to dance with her, though he didn't fancy himself much of a dancer. And then he wondered if she might even consider going to the ball with him. It might be the only chance he ever got to see a former president of the United States in the flesh. He didn't have a suit, but maybe he could get hold of one some way.

While he was thinking along these lines Jack walked right up to him.

"It's mighty hot to stand outdoors and read a newspaper," Jack said.

Strate started, surprised by Jack's sudden appearance.

"You ought to be a little more careful about who you let slip up on you, too," Jack said. "One of our friends is in town."

"How did you know?" Strate said. He didn't see how Jack could already have heard of the shooting.

Then Jack told him about his little set-to with Tollie.

"You let him get away, did you?" Strate said, smiling.

Jack didn't return the smile. "You haven't done so well yourself," he said.

"You don't know the half of it," Strate said. He told him about the shooting at the beach, leaving out only the part about Sally.

"You went swimming late at night, all alone?" Jack was incredulous.

"There was someone with me," Strate admitted.

"Who?"

"A woman." Strate wasn't smiling now. He was not about to bandy Sally's name around in conversation, not even with Jack.

Jack understood. "I see. And while you were out there, someone took a shot at you."

"Shots," Strate said. "More than one."

"And I take it that you're sure it was not an irate husband."

Strate just looked at him.

"You're sure, then. Well, given the time that it happened, it couldn't have been Tollie. He was pretty well occupied for the better part of the night. It must have been one of the others."

"Between the two of us, we seem to have gotten them fairly stirred up. I'm sure Tollie didn't know you, or why he was being followed, though."

"No, but it will be enough to make him suspicious."

"We won't worry about him, then. Anyway, I know where we can find Patch. He's working on the docks."

"How do you know that?"

"I just know it. We can go down there late this afternoon and follow him after he gets off work. If we get a chance, we can grab him and hang on to him until he tells us where the money is."

"I didn't do such a good job of following Tollie," Jack pointed out.

"Maybe not, but you may have to be the one who does the following. Patch knows me, and this red hair of mine makes me stick out.

"You can wear a hat."

"Let's just see if we can locate him. He's loading cotton."

"We can locate him, then."

"Good. I'll meet you here late this afternoon and we'll go looking."

"I'll be here," Jack said.

Tollie and Patch had met earlier, before going to work. When Patch told him about Seth's sighting of Strate, Tollie said, "Somebody was following me last night. I was out for a little entertainment, and someone got on my trail."

"Who was it?" Patch said.

"Don't have no idea. Never got a good look at him, but I finally had to take a few shots at him to discourage him."

"Maybe you showed too much money around," Patch suggested. "I told you to keep that bankroll out of sight while we were here."

Tollie's temper flared slightly. "Look, that money is mine, and I'm goin' to enjoy it. I didn't flash it around, just spent a little bit of it. I got a right to do that."

Patch didn't want to argue with Tollie. There was no point in it.

"Some of these places around here are bound to be full of men with sharp eyes," he said. "They can see money from a long way off."

"Not where I was," Tollie insisted. But then he began to wonder about that little girl he had been with. Maybe that was part of their game there, to single out one of the customers and follow him after he left, then roll him for his money.

He didn't say anything to Patch about what he was thinking, but he thought he might pay another visit to that place and just see what happened. If anyone followed him again, he'd know better how to deal with them the next time.

Then Patch told him that they had to work fast, that they had only a couple of days to get their job done.

"That's fine with me," Tollie said. "I'm already tired of this cotton jammin'."

"You and me both," Patch said.

Tollie worked hard that day, but he also took time to talk whenever he could to Fairly Harper and Edgar Freeman and whoever else would listen about the injustice of their pay and situation. He laid it on thick again about how the white men did the same job for better pay, and how the bosses didn't care.

He must have done a good job of it, because by the end of the day, even Harper was saying that there was some truth in Tollie's version of what was going on.

Edgar Freeman, of course, had been in agreement all along, and he began talking along the same lines to some of his friends, who all agreed with what he had to say.

"White men always want to keep us down," Tollie said. "Always want to make sure we don't have as good a house as they do, or as good a horse. Make us live in our own part of town, have our own clubs, our own stores, everything like that. Think we ain't good enough to talk to them on the street or live close by."

"Amen," Edgar said, and Fairly Harper had to admit that much of what Tollie said was on the mark.

"You brush up against a white man on the street," Fairly said, "and you find your ass in jail in ten minutes. You try to walk in his front door and you get to jail even faster."

"That's why they don't want to pay us a decent living," Edgar said. "They afraid we come up to the front door."

"We could do somethin' about that if we wanted to," Tollie said. "We could get some of that money they don't want us to have."

Everyone who heard him agreed that it would be a fine idea.

Patch was busy, too.

He kept up his line of talk to Radford and Taylor, but he made sure that others heard him as well.

Nearly everyone was sympathetic to him.

"It's the niggers that're keeping us down," he said, resting his arms on a cotton bale. "They know they can get our jobs if we try to get better conditions. The bosses won't dare to close down the docks."

"That's right," someone chimed in. "If they closed down the docks, the whole town'd go to the dogs."

"What're we supposed to do about it, though?" Taylor wondered.

"Don't give 'em the chance. If they try to take our jobs, we show 'em where they belong," Patch said. "No nigger can stand up to a white man in a fair fight."

Even as he mouthed the words, he laughed inwardly. He had seen Tollie take on as many as three white men at a time and send them flying heels over headbones.

Probably the others had seen similar things, but that didn't matter. When it came to their jobs, they were willing to believe what they wanted to believe.

"You're damned right they can't," someone said. "We ought to show them who the real workers around here are."

"That's right," Patch said. "If we all stand together, they can't whip us, and they'll never load a single ship if we face them down."

There was not a single dissenting voice, and Patch went back to work well satisfied with himself. This kind of thing was exactly what the Colonel was looking for. If they could drive a wedge between the black and white workers, the riots that the Colonel had mentioned were a distinct possibility, whether or not they pointed out the viciousness of the blacks. And if there were riots, there was not much chance that the blacks would be getting any of the whites' jobs. And all of the confusion would help cover all of them in the aftermath of the Colonel's real mission.

Patch was convinced that things were going along very well.

Colonel Peter Benson had a leisurely breakfast at a waterfront café. It was not the kind of place he preferred to frequent, being somewhat run-down and dirty, but he himself did not appear as he preferred to these days, dressed as he was in dingy linen and an old suit that was shiny at the seat and knees and frayed around the cuffs.

Neither was the Colonel wearing his wooden hand. It was one distinguishing mark that set him apart from everyone, and being set apart was one risk he could not afford to take. Still, he did not want to appear to have only one hand; that, too, could set him apart. He had an old shirt with a cotton glove sewn to the sleeve. The glove was stuffed with cotton on the inside, and while the false hand did not seem extremely real, it was good enough to fool a casual observer. Colonel Benson was sure that no one would take more than a casual interest in a shabby man in shabby clothing who kept to the poorer part of town.

Like Strate, Benson was reading the article concerning Grant's arrival. He noted with interest that Sheridan would be accompanying Grant, which he had expected, his sources being what they were.

There was another article, one to which Strate had paid no particular attention, that told of the visit to Galveston by Norris Cuney.

Benson smiled as he read it. Cuney was unlikely to be invited to the grand ball at the Pavilion, but Benson knew that the Negro leader would be meeting with Grant somewhere in the city. Benson's plans were beginning to take shape.

After breakfast Benson strolled back to his hotel. He hated being cooped up there, but there was nothing for him to do except wait. Later, when it was necessary, he would go into action.

He reflected that he hadn't told even Patch the exact truth about what they were doing in Galveston. He trusted Patch, had trusted him and depended on him for years after the war, when they were more like outlaws than anything.

Benson didn't really like to think back on those days. He had come out of them with a great deal of money but with a tainted reputation. It had taken several years for the money to overcome the taint, but eventually it had, as he'd believed it always would.

He had, in fact, a great deal more money than anyone realized, even Patch. He had shared the spoils with his men, but the sharing had been far from equal. The mysterious backers that he had mentioned to Patch in Houston did not really exist. Benson did not have backers. He had put up the money for this venture himself. It had been his own project from the beginning.

But the lie about the backers had not been the only lie.

There were others, but the truth had been mixed in. Benson himself was not always sure any longer when he was telling the truth and when he was lying. He had lied too much and too often.

It was true that he did not want the black dockworkers to take the jobs of the whites if there was a strike, but that was only a part of it, a small part.

What really bothered him was the growing power of blacks in the state, particularly the growing power of Norris Cuney.

Cuney was exactly the kind of man that Benson feared: clever, an excellent politician, and a man who knew how to appeal to both blacks and whites. The kind of man who was capable of seizing and keeping power.

Benson didn't want to see Cuney become even more successful than he already was. Disorder and even rioting on the docks would be a setback for him, and Benson wanted to stir up the dockworkers any way he could, exactly as he had told Patch.

He had never told Patch why he hated the black men, however.

He had never told anyone.

He had heard and sympathized with the story of the death of Tollie's parents at the hands of the black soldiers, and he felt he understood Tollie as well as he would ever understand any black man, but he felt no liking for him.

Tollie's story was nothing like Benson's own.

Benson's story had happened long before the war, had happened when Benson was only a child. Ten years old? Benson no longer remembered, if he ever had, but he must have been about that age, the age at which a boy thinks his mother is the most beautiful woman in the world and his father the most wonderful man.

The truth was that his mother was rather plain, his father quite old. He must have been around seventy at the time, and Benson had been the child of his old age.

Because he was so glad to have a child, especially a son, the old man took special pains with Benson, teaching him all about their little farm, taking him fishing whenever there was a chance, spending much more time with him than most fathers of that era ever spent with their sons.

Benson idolized him.

Benson's mother was much younger than her husband. She was, in fact, his second wife, the first having died of cholera thirty years before the old man married for the second time. She had come from a very poor family, and her parents regarded the elderly Mr. Benson as a fine catch, even if he was getting along in years.

She found no satisfaction in the marriage, not even in the son they had managed to have together, but she managed to find satisfaction in other ways.

Benson had found out about those ways when he was ten years old.

His father had gone to town to have some harvest tools mended, and Benson had stayed behind for some reason or other. He couldn't remember why. Usually when his father went to town, he went with him.

But not this time.

There were two slaves on the farm, a man and his wife. The man was nothing remarkable, not particularly strong, certainly not handsome by the boy's standards, but a hard worker.

The wife was a hard worker, too, and they had a tiny one-room cabin about a hundred yards from the Benson house.

Benson didn't know where the wife was that day, nor did he ever find out. It never seemed to matter.

His mother had gone out to the barn to gather the eggs, or so she had said. For some reason Benson went to find her. He thought he recalled cutting his finger with the pocketknife his father had given him a few weeks before, but he might have been wrong.

When he got to the barn, he heard a strange sound, like someone being hurt, or so he thought. It sounded as if someone were moaning in pain.

He didn't call out.

He was too scared.

But at the same time he was curious.

He pushed open the heavy wooden barn door.

He could still remember what he saw then, remember with all the clarity of the daylight around him.

He could remember the way the light came in through the cracks in the barn walls and roof, shafts of sunlight with motes of dust and tiny pieces of straw spinning in them.

He could remember his mother lying back in a pile of straw, her dress up under her armpits, her white legs in the air.

He could remember the black man on top of her, straining and groaning as he pushed himself into her.

It was his mother who was making most of the noise.

Benson turned away and walked back to the house. His cut finger was forgotten, but tears were running down his cheeks. He was not making a sound, but he was crying steadily, and he cried for a long time.

He never told anyone what he saw, but he never let his mother kiss him after that (not that she minded), and he never looked at his father with respect again. The bond they had shared was gone, as if it had never been, and his father never knew why.

The slaves' cabin had burned one night six months later. Both the man and the wife had died in the fire, and no one ever knew that the front door had been propped shut or that the window had been nailed down a few days before, when no one was there.

No one except Peter Benson, and he never told.

Since that time he had done what he could to thwart the cause of the freed slaves, and he had been terribly disappointed in the outcome of the war. He had kept his own war going after that, and when finally he had accumulated enough money, he had vowed that one day he would do something big, something that would make Negro men sorry for what they had done to him.

Now, here in Galveston, he had his chance.

He had told Patch that they were going to assassinate Grant.

Well, if they did, that would be fine. Grant had cost the South the war as much as anyone.

But Grant was not the one Benson really wanted.

The one he really wanted was Norris Cuney, and if there was any way in Benson's power to arrange it, Cuney was going to die.

His death would set the cause of the black man in Texas back for years, and Benson would be the one responsible.

The idea warmed him like the sun.

And after Cuney was dead, a strong leader would arise out of the chaos in Galveston. That leader would be Colonel Peter Benson, who, he devoutly hoped, would then be well on his way to becoming the next governor of the state of Texas.

Chapter Fifteen

The afternoon had become increasingly hot and muggy. Strate pulled his bandanna out of his back pocket and mopped his face with it.

He and Jack were standing in an alleyway across from the docks, watching a ship named the *Ellen Scott* being loaded by a crew of men, which included one with a patch on his right eye.

"That's him, all right," Strate said. "I'll never forget that fella."

Jack had been able to locate Patch by asking around among some of the black workers on the dock. One of them had told him about seeing the man with the eye patch just the day before and had given him the name of the ship. Fortunately, though he hadn't done so deliberately, Jack had not asked anyone from the ship where Tollie was loading. That ship, the *Fox Trader,* was a little farther down the docks.

"They should be knocking off soon," Strate said.

He wondered which of the men was Sally's father. He was sorry he wasn't going to be visiting Sally's house to ask about Patch, but he had decided to act as soon as possible. Talking to Mr. Radford would only delay matters, and he didn't think he would learn anything about Patch that he needed to know. He wanted to see Sally again, and he would, but not until he had his money, or what was left of it, back.

After a few minutes the bare-chested men crammed the last of the bales into the hold, and work was halted for the day.

Several of the men stood around to talk, letting the breeze dry the sweat on their hot and salty bodies. One of them was Patch, who seemed especially earnest as he engaged several men in conversation. Strate strained his ears, but he couldn't make out what was being said.

One of the men waved his hands to make a point, and Patch nodded vigorously in agreement. All of them seemed agitated about something, and the conversation continued to be animated.

Finally the group broke up and Patch slipped on his shirt. Strate watched from the shadow of the alley, and when Patch strode away, Strate and Jack slipped out to follow him.

They gave him a block's head start, and there were plenty of people around to give them cover. Patch stood out from the crowd, and Strate was sure he and Jack could follow without any danger of being sighted.

The trouble occurred within three blocks of their starting out, however.

There was a large group of people standing around on both sides of the street, as well as in the middle. There was lots of shouting and gesticulating. Strate didn't know what was happening, but something clearly was. Patch walked into the middle of the group and vanished.

Strate and Jack picked up the pace, breaking through the fringes of the group.

In the middle of the street was a huge alligator. It looked to Strate to be ten or twelve feet long.

Two men had it lassoed, one with a rope around its jaws, the other with a rope around its tail.

The gator was not pleased with its situation. It was lashing its tail, causing the man at its rear to have considerable difficulty hanging on. It was also trying to open its powerful jaws. The man in front was trying to keep the rope drawn tight, but he was not quite strong enough.

The crowd was shouting encouragement.

"Give 'em hell, Jackson! He ain't nothin' but a baby!" one man called out.

"That's right," shouted another, "but watch out if his momma comes along to help him out!"

The men were clearly struggling to clear the gator off the street, but they were not having much success.

The crowd was on the side of the gator.

"Watch it that he don't bite you on the nose, Jackson! You can't afford to lose none of that beauty of yours!"

Strate noticed that the man at the front of the gator had a long, pointed nose that now was very red.

"You let that tail hit you, Tommy, and you're long gone!"

The gator's tail gave an extremely vicious jerk, and the rope burned through Tommy's hands, but he didn't let go.

As interesting as the alligator was, Strate was more interested in finding Patch. He looked through the crowd but didn't see him.

Jack nudged him in the ribs with his elbow.

Strate looked, and Jack gestured. Patch was across the street and moving away from them.

They shoved through the laughing, yelling men and got across the street.

Patch had already turned the corner, but they were sure of the direction. They ran to catch up.

They barely made it in time. Patch was entering the door of the boardinghouse.

"That's it," Strate said. "That's where he's staying."

"We didn't grab him, though," Jack said.

"At least we know where he is. We can go in after him."

"That might not be such a good idea. You never know who might be there. I don't think he's going to give us your money just because he likes the way we look."

Jack was right. They couldn't just go into the house after Patch, but Strate didn't want to have to wait outside until Patch took a notion to go out. He might not do that until morning, when it was time to go to work.

"There's got to be a way to get to him," Strate said.

"I don't know what it is," Jack said.

"Maybe I can help you boys out," said a deep voice behind them.

Strate recognized it instantly.

It was Tollie.

Tollie took them up an outside back stairway. They didn't particularly want to go with him, but he was holding a Smith and Wesson revolver in his right hand, and he didn't look as if he wanted any arguments.

Patch opened the door when they got to the top of the stairs as if he had been waiting for them.

It turned out that he had.

"I thought it was that son of a bitch when I spotted him in that crowd," Patch said.

"Sure enough, it was," Tollie said. "And I bet his partner here is the same one that followed me last night. Here I was, thinkin' I was gonna have to go back to that house tonight and look for him, and he shows up with our old buddy instead."

"Pretty obliging of him, all right," Patch said. "Why don't you two fellas just have a seat while we decide what to do with you."

There wasn't much room, and there was only one chair, but Strate and Jack sat. Jack took the chair, and Strate sat on the bed, which had a cover that was none too clean. And the mattress was lumpy.

Tollie stood and looked at them. "Move the chair a little closer to the bed," he said.

Jack obeyed. "You gentlemen must have eyes in the backs of your heads," he said as he scraped the chair across the floor.

"Nothing like that," Patch said. "I spotted your friend there while you were looking at that alligator. Tollie was in the crowd, too, and when I saw him, I told him to hang back and see where you were going. And now here you are, right where you wanted to be."

They weren't where they wanted to be at all, but neither Strate nor Jack mentioned that fact.

"I just wanted my money back," Strate said. "You can give it to me now, and we'll leave quietly."

Patch laughed. "That would be mighty nice of me, wouldn't it? But I've got kind of attached to that money. It's almost like it belongs to me now."

He took a pillowcase and began tearing it into strips. When he was done, he tied Jack and Strate's hands behind their backs.

Then he gagged them. The pillowcase tasted to Strate like the inside of a musty closet.

"Want me to shoot 'em?" Tollie said.

"Too much noise. And too much trouble getting them back down those stairs. We'll let them walk down. Then we'll kill them."

He looked at Strate, and for the first time he seemed to notice that Strate was wearing a pistol. He walked over and slipped the Peacemaker out of its holster.

"Nice weapon," he said, looking it over. Then he handed the gun to Tollie, who took it with his left hand and slid it in his belt. His right hand, holding his own pistol, never wavered.

Strate and Jack looked at each other. Though he couldn't talk, Jack's look said clearly that he was sorry he'd ever gotten involved with Strate and his lost money.

Strate, for his part, was beginning to regret the whole business. It was only money, after all. But then, he'd worked hard for it, and he didn't want to have someone just take it from him. He wished he'd met Sally Radford sooner, however. He would have liked to spend more time with her, gotten to know her better. He was surprised, in fact, to realize how strongly he felt about her, now that it looked as if he would never see her again.

But that was the wrong tack to take. He would see her again. He had been in bad fixes before, and he had always gotten out of them. He would get out of this one, too.

How he would get out he didn't know, and Tollie and Patch were not going to make it easy.

"We'll wait until it gets full dark," Patch was saying. "Then we can walk them down the stairs and get them to the dock. Down there, there won't be anyone to bother us. We can take care of them without any trouble."

"You think they know anything about—" Tollie began.

"They don't know anything about anything," Patch said, cutting him off short. "The less said, the better."

"Hell, we're gonna kill 'em, anyhow," Tollie said.

"That's right, but they're going to die without knowing our business."

After that no one said very much.

Jack and Strate sat where they were and tried their bonds with no success, while the sweat formed in their hair and rolled down their faces. Patch had closed the window of the room, and the heat and humidity were almost intolerable.

They didn't have to sit for long. It was already late, and darkness came all too soon.

"How do we get 'em to the dock without anybody seein' us?" Tollie wanted to know.

"We'll stick to the alleys," Patch said. "Down there, no one will care what we're doing." He looked at Jack and Strate. "You two get up."

They stood.

Tollie motioned them over to the door with a twitch of the Smith and Wesson. They went where he directed.

Patch opened the door. "Out," he said.

They went out onto the small porch and began to descend the stairs. When they got to the bottom, they stopped, finding themselves confronted by Seth.

"Well, well, well," the mush-mouthed man said. "Looky here. What you gonna do with 'em, Patch?"

"I'm glad you're here," Patch said. "I'll let you and Tollie handle it. I want to go tell the Colonel that he doesn't have anything to worry about from these two anymore."

"What you want me to do?"

"Take them down to the docks. Then you and Tollie knock them in the head with your pistols and throw them in the bay. Let them drown. If anybody finds them, maybe they'll think they got in a fight, knocked each other silly, and fell in. Not that I give a damn what anybody thinks about them, as long as they're not in our way tomorrow night.''

Seth smiled and pulled out a pistol, a Smith and Wesson like Tollie's, the Schofield model .45, Strate noticed.

''I like that idea,'' Seth said. He looked at Strate. ''This here fella likes to go swimmin'. Too bad he ain't got no naked lady to go in with him this time.''

Strate would have liked to stomp Seth into the street, but he made no move. This was not the time or the place.

Tollie prodded them with his pistol, and they walked down the alley.

They reached the docks without any interruption. Strate hadn't really hoped for any. It was dark, the alleys were deserted, and those on the streets in this part of town were used to minding their own business.

During the late afternoon Strate had looked at the tall masts of the ships and thought that they appeared graceful and serene. Now, silhouetted against the night sky, the spars and rigging looked ghostly and threatening.

Tollie stopped them at the end of the last alley while he stepped out to look the area over.

There didn't appear to be anyone around, and he came back to stand beside them. ''Let's go,'' he said.

Strate's mouth was so dry from the gag that he couldn't have spoken had the gag been removed. If Tollie thought that he was going to walk quietly out to the edge of the dock and stand there while they hit him in the head, then Tollie was in for a surprise.

Making a sudden quick turn, Strate threw his back against Tollie, his fingers reaching for the pistol in Tollie's belt. The pillowcase was not tied as tightly as a rope would have been, and his fingers still had feeling in them.

Before Tollie quite realized what was going on, Strate had jerked the pistol free and was running out of the alley.

Jack, no fool, was right behind him.

Seth and Tollie both fired at them, the two shots sounding as one.

Strate had no idea where one of the slugs went, but one of them ricocheted off the street, striking a spark by Strate's left boot.

Strate ran faster, as Seth and Tollie fired again.

The gangplank was still down to one of the ships, and Strate ran up it. Jack was not far behind. They ducked down behind the railing as shots thunked into the side of the ship.

Without being told, Jack had his back to Strate and was working on the pillowcase. The knots were too hard; he couldn't budge them.

A man appeared from somewhere on the ship. A watchman, Strate guessed. He was carrying a knife.

"What the bloody hell is goin' on here?" he yelled in an accent Strate had never heard before.

A bullet hit him square in the middle of the face. He wouldn't be doing any more yelling. He pitched backward, the knife falling from his limp fingers.

Jack went for the knife.

Tollie and Seth were heading for the gangplank.

There was really no place to hide on the sailing vessel, but the hold was open. Strate dived in, followed by Jack.

The hold was partially loaded with cotton bales, which was softer than some things would have been, but not as soft as Strate might have wanted. He rolled over on his stomach, and Jack slipped the knife between his wrists and slit the pillowcase.

Somehow Strate had managed to hang on to the pistol. It was very dark in the hold, but he could see the opening as a lighter patch of darkness. He braced himself against a cotton bale and aimed the pistol at the opening.

Nothing happened for a few minutes. He could hear Tollie and Seth walking around on the deck.

"Where the hell are they?" Tollie rumbled.

"I don't know, but we better get outa here," Seth said. "Somebody's bound to come, and when they find that dead man . . ."

"If they get away, Patch'll have our balls. And the Colonel . . ."

"We tell 'em we did the job. Those two don't know about the Pavilion."

"They know where Patch is stayin'."

"I'll tell him the law followed us back, that they got suspicious. We can stay somewhere else for a day."

Tollie didn't say anything. Maybe he was thinking.

Strate debated whether to attack them, but the pillowcase had cut off at least a little of his circulation and his fingers were beginning to sting and tingle. He knew he couldn't shoot straight.

"Somebody's comin'," Seth said.

"Clear out," Tollie said.

Strate heard their footsteps leave the deck and hit the gangplank.

Shortly after that, he thought he heard voices on the dock, but no one came on the ship. When he was finally sure that they were safe, he put down the gun and took the knife from Jack. He cut Jack's bonds and gag. Then Jack removed Strate's gag.

Strate needed a drink of water in the worst way. His tongue felt like a swollen cork.

Neither he nor Jack could say a word, but there was nothing he wanted to say, not then.

He needed time to think things through. Five thousand dollars was a lot of money, but it wasn't worth getting killed for.

Chapter Sixteen

They couldn't go back to the whorehouse; Tollie had made it clear that he knew who had followed him from there. Jack, however, would not have been welcome in Strate's hotel.

It was Strate's idea to go back to Patch's room. "They won't be looking for us there, and if they tell him to stay away, maybe he won't even go back." He paused significantly. "He might leave the money there."

"Or all three of them might come back there to pick it up," Jack said.

"If they do, we'll be ready for them." Strate hefted the pistol in his hand. He had thought about it, and he wanted his money back. More than that, he wanted them to pay for the beating he had taken, the shots that had been fired at him and Sally, and all the trouble he had taken in finding them.

Jack was still holding the knife he had picked up on the ship. It was a wicked-looking weapon with an eight-inch blade that he could have shaved with had he wanted to. "All right," he said. He had a score to settle with them now. He could still taste the gag in his mouth. "But let's get a drink somewhere first."

"We can get a drink later. First let's go after that money, before they have time to clean it out."

Strate started down the alley, and Jack followed, moving fast.

They reached the boardinghouse without incident and climbed the outside stairs. Patch's door was locked, but Jack easily pried it open with the blade of his new knife and they slipped inside.

The room was dark and hot, the window still down. They didn't open it, nor did they turn on the gaslight. They didn't want anyone to know they were there.

Jack stood by the closed door, his knife at the ready, while Strate searched the room.

There wasn't much to search: a deal dresser with glass drawer knobs, one of which was missing; a battered carpet bag; the lumpy bed; and a washstand with a pitcher and bowl on it.

All Strate found was several shirts, some pants, and a handkerchief in the dresser. In the washstand were a filthy towel and a washrag, nothing more.

"Look under the rug," Jack said.

There was a frayed and faded piece of carpet in the center of the room. Strate pulled it up by the corner and peeled it back. Dust flew everywhere. It was clear that the carpet had not been moved for months, probably years.

"Check that mattress out again," Jack said. "He could have cut it and stuffed the money inside."

Strate checked again, but there was still no money, and no sign that the mattress had ever been cut.

"Damn," he said. "He must have the money on him."

"Or he hid it someplace. Or put it in a bank," Jack said.

"Damn."

"We can wait here and hope he comes back," Jack said.

"We might as well. I'd bet that Tollie and his pal have warned him away, though. For all they know, there might be twelve policemen waiting here for them.

"In that case, it's just about the safest place we can be right now," Jack said. "Why don't we have the police here, anyway?"

"It's none of their business," Strate said.

"I see," Jack said. He didn't see, but he didn't want to

pursue the matter. Strate would tell him if he wanted to.

"We might as well spend the night here," Strate said. "We can take turns keeping watch, just in case."

"Then what do we do?"

"I've been thinking about that. They were careful not to tell us anything, but I think they did, anyway."

Jack thought back on what had been said. "Patch mentioned that he didn't want us in the way tomorrow night," he said. "That's not a lot of help. That could mean anything."

"Put it with what Tollie said while we were hiding in the hold," Strate told him.

"You mean, you were listening to what they said? I was just trying to keep from pissing in my pants."

Strate laughed. "I had the pistol back and my hands loose. I was hoping they'd find us."

"Not me," Jack said. "What did he say?"

"Something about how we didn't know about the Pavilion."

"Well," Jack said, "they're right. I don't know a thing about it."

"Maybe not," Strate said. "But I do."

"Are you going to tell me?"

"There was an article in the paper today. I hardly glanced at it, but it said there was going to be a big ball at the Electric Pavilion tomorrow night.

"That's nice," Jack said. "They forgot to send me my invitation."

"You don't need one. Everyone's invited."

"I don't imagine they would want me to be there," Jack said.

Strate finally got the point. "You may be right, but I think we ought to be there, anyway. That bunch has something planned."

"You think they might stick up the crowd?"

"Could be. They seem to like taking money from folks. But I don't think they'd try that with this crowd. President Grant's going to be there, along with five thousand other people."

"What on earth would President Grant be doing in Galveston?"

"He likes to travel," Strate said.

"You think they'd try to rob *him?*"

"They might. One thing's for sure. They'll be there, if what we overheard is right. And if they're going to be there, I want to be there. And this time there won't be any mistakes. We'll be the ones with the upper hand."

"There'll be a lot of people. Five thousand. How are we going to pick them out of that many people?"

Strate remembered that he hadn't seen Mush-mouth at the greased-pig scramble, and there hadn't been near five thousand people there then.

"I don't know," he said. "We'll just have to do it."

"All right," Jack said. "If that's the best idea you've got, then we'll have to try it."

"It's the best idea I've got. I have to admit that my other ideas haven't been so hot, though."

"Not your fault," Jack said. "Is there any water in that pitcher?"

Strate picked up the pitcher from the washstand and shook it.

"A little," he said.

"Think it would be all right to drink it?"

"I don't see why not." Strate handed the pitcher to Jack. "You first."

Jack took a healthy swallow from the pitcher, then passed it back.

Strate drank. The water felt cool going down his throat.

"Who gets the first watch?" Jack asked.

"I'll take it," Strate said. "I'm not sure I can sleep on that bed, anyway."

"It's worth a try," Jack said. He walked over and stretched out on it. "Wake me up when you're ready."

The bed might have been uncomfortable, but Jack was asleep in minutes. He'd had a hard night and a harder day.

Tollie and Seth met Patch as he came from the Colonel's hotel.

"You dump those two in the bay?" Patch said.

"Right," Tollie said. He was the spokesman. Seth was too excitable and might get things tangled up.

"They put up much of a fight?"

"Not much."

"Good. The Colonel's glad to have that settled. He didn't want to have them getting in our way tomorrow night."

"We had a little trouble, though," Tollie said.

Patch was instantly alert. "What kind?"

"Nothing bad. There was a little disturbance on the docks, and the police followed us back to your room. I think they were suspicious."

"And you led them to my room?" Patch was getting angry already.

Seth decided to speak up. "It was my . . . my . . . my . . ."

"It's his room, too," Tollie said. "He wanted to get a few things, not leave anything there that would identify you two."

It was a weak story, but Tollie hadn't been able to think of anything better. Patch seemed to buy it, however.

"Hell," he said, "it's only for one night. We can go to your place."

Tollie didn't think that was a good idea. Some of the waterfront hotels would accept both blacks and whites, but Tollie wasn't sure about his.

"We'll have to risk it," Patch said. "I'm not about to tell the Colonel that the police are snooping around. Are you?"

"No," Tollie admitted.

"Then let's go. When we get there, I'll tell you about tomorrow."

Tollie's room was even less attractive than the one Patch and Seth had shared, but at least no one objected to the presence of the two white men. For that matter, no one had even noticed their entrance. The desk clerk was asleep in a chair, and there was no one else in the dingy lobby to see them enter.

"What about tomorrow?" Tollie said when they were

inside the room. He didn't want to give Patch a chance to begin asking questions about what had happened on the docks. Tollie was sure that Seth would make a mistake within the first two minutes if Patch questioned them closely.

"Tomorrow we go to work as usual. Seth goes out on the Strand. Spreads his rumors wherever he can. We keep them going on the docks."

Tollie nodded. That was simple enough.

"Then, tomorrow night, we meet at the Pavilion."

Tollie nodded again. He already knew that much. "What do we do then?"

"There's going to be a big party there, but we're not going to the party," Patch said.

Tollie knew about the party, too. He was beginning to wonder when Patch was going to get to the point.

Seth was wondering as well, but he didn't say anything. He didn't want to risk calling attention to how nervous he was.

"There'll be a lot of people there," Patch went on. "But we're only interested in two of them."

Now they were getting somewhere, Tollie thought. "Which two?" he said.

"One of them is General U.S. Grant," Patch said. "You've heard of him, I guess."

"I guess," Tollie said. "Who's the other one?"

"Norris Cuney."

Tollie had never heard of Norris Cuney, or if he had, he didn't remember it. Benson had told Patch about Cuney, but he hadn't mentioned him to Tollie, who didn't keep up with politics. The subject had no interest for him."

"Who's Cuney?" he said.

"He's a black leader here in Texas."

"All right. Why are we interested in those two?"

"We're going to assassinate them," Patch said.

Colonel Benson was feeling good. His plans were going well, and the only flies in the ointment had been eliminated. By this time tomorrow night, Grant and Cuney would be dead, and he would be well on his way to the governorship.

He would move into a better hotel tomorrow, as if he had just come into the city, and he would attend the ball. He would be there when the killing was done, and he would be the only one who knew what was really going on. He had come a long way from stealing horses, he thought, remembering the way it had been. The long, cold nights on the run; the dreary days in the saddle with rain running down the neck of his slicker; the constant fear that the next day would be his last, his life ended by the bullet from a lawman's gun. It had been a long road, but he had made it. Now he was going to reap the rewards.

He had finally taken Patch into his confidence and told him who their real target was. Patch would tell the others, but it was too late now for them to let anyone know. What could go wrong in only one day?

The South had lost the war, but he had survived that.

He had lost his hand, and he had survived that as well.

He had money, and he had power. He almost had respect.

After tomorrow night he would have that, too.

Of course, there was a little more to his plan than what he had told Patch, but there was no need to tell every single detail. Patch would find out soon enough, as would Tollie and Seth.

After all, a man had to keep some secrets for himself.

Seth had finally spoken up.

"Assass . . . assass . . . assass . . ."

"Assassinate," Patch said calmly.

"That means . . . means . . ."

"It means we're going to kill them," Patch said. "That's what it means, I guess."

Seth was sputtering so much that he couldn't even make a coherent sound. Tollie took over.

"Why?" he said. "Why are we gonna kill General Grant and this Cuney fella?"

"Because the Colonel wants us to," Patch said, thinking that he would give an answer they could understand.

"Why does he want us to?"

"Dammit!" Patch said. "Don't you know what Grant did to the Colonel?"

"He won the war," Tollie said.

"Wasn't that enough?"

Tollie guessed that it was. "But what about that other fella? That Cuney? What did he ever do?"

"He's a black man. The Colonel doesn't like blacks. You ought to know that. Besides, he's trying to take over the state government."

Seth had heard about Cuney, though Tollie didn't appear to have known. Seth had been spreading rumors about Cuney for several days, and they seemed to agree with what Patch was telling them. He could understand the Colonel's motives, but he was still upset by the whole thing. He was used to simple crimes, like stealing horses or robbing some stranger that they encountered on the road. He didn't understand about assassination.

"I sure do hope the Colonel is planning to pay us for this," Tollie said. "I don't think we've done anything this dangerous for him before."

Patch had known the issue of pay would come up, and he had been careful to ask about it. The Colonel had promised five thousand a man without blinking an eye.

"You know how much we got from that fella on the trail?" he said. "Well, we'll get that much more. For each one of us."

That got even Seth's attention, and calmed him down a bit. "Who's gonna do . . . do . . . it?" he said.

"Tollie and me," Patch said. "You can be the lookout."

That was just fine with Seth.

Chapter Seventeen

The train that Grant and Sheridan and their party rode into Galveston was no finer than the one ridden by Strate and Jack, but the private car which Grant and Sheridan rode was in no way like the one the other two had traveled in.

The car's windows were curtained with black velvet drapes, drawn back and held by ties of thick gold cord. The seats were covered with a plush red material that was soft and yielding. The wood paneling was polished to a high shine. If it had been raining, which it was not, the car would not have leaked a drop; and if it had been cold, which it decidedly was not, the potbellied stoves at each end of the car would have kept the passengers warm and comfortable.

Sheridan, Little Phil as he was sometimes known, was not one of the world's most prepossessing men. His receding hairline gave him a pronounced widow's peak, and his weak chin was not helped by his thick mustache. No one who saw him would guess that he was one of the bravest men Grant had ever known, and one of his most trusted associates.

"This journey through Texas has been most enlightening," Sheridan observed to Grant, raising his voice to be heard above the clacking of the train wheels. "But it has not been dangerous."

"Sometimes the president exaggerates," Grant res-

141

ponded, not mentioning that their final stop, in Galveston, was supposed to be the most likely spot for trouble.

"Well, it is an interesting state, take it all in all," Sheridan said. "Though not entirely a pleasant one. The climate, for one thing, is almost unbearable. And the very bugs that creep into your room are equipped with the most fearsome stings."

Sheridan had experienced an encounter with a small scorpion in his boot two nights before and had not yet recovered.

"All in all," he said, "I believe that if I owned both hell and Texas, I would rent out Texas and live in hell."

Grant laughed. Sheridan had a way with words, all right.

"If I were you," Grant said, "I'd try that line on some pretty lady at the ball they're having for us."

Sheridan grinned, pleased with himself. "I will," he said. "I certainly will."

The two men sat in silence for a few minutes, listening to the wheels on the rails and looking out the windows at the bay and the blue sky.

"This Cuney we are to meet," Sheridan said. "Is he to be trusted?"

Grant was not the best judge of character, as his administration had shown, but he still thought of himself as shrewd when it came to recognizing a man's good and bad traits.

"I believe so," he said. "I believe that his word will be his bond."

"And that this strike can be averted?"

"If not the strike, then the violence that it threatens. No man likes the thought of violence less than I, and I hope to be able to say a good word."

Sheridan was not a politician like Grant, and he had never mastered the art of talking like one. Still, he thought he got the gist of what Grant was saying.

"And if there is a strike and violence does occur?"

"Then I have done what I could," Grant said. "And that was all I promised to do. After that I hope to be left alone in peace to write my memoirs and enjoy what is left of my life."

"A worthy ambition," Sheridan said, though his own ambitions still lay in military advancement. The idea about writing a memoir appealed to him, however, and he thought that there was a great deal he could tell the world if he so chose. Maybe someday he would have the time to do so.

The two men looked out the windows as the train finished its trip across the bay.

Patch, Tollie, and Seth separated early in the morning, each to his appointed task.

Patch did have one final bit of information for them, however.

"The Colonel wants us to meet at the Pavilion about nine o'clock," he said. "By the tower. He'll tell us what to do after that."

"We won't be goin' to the ball?" Tollie said.

"No. What we have to do will be done somewhere else. But the Colonel will be there. When he meets us, he'll give us the plan."

"And we just keep stirrin' the pot," Tollie said.

"That's right. For the rest of the day. After that we get out of here. Fast."

"I don't suppose the Colonel mentioned how we were supposed to do that, did he?" Tollie said.

"No," Patch said. "But I'm sure he'll tell us tonight."

"That's good," Tollie said. "Because it just came to me that here we are on an island. No way off but by train or boat. No bridge, 'less you count that railroad bridge, and ain't no way we're gonna walk across that thing. Don't strike me as a good place to do a 'ssassanation."

"Me . . . me, neither," Seth said.

Patch, who liked to think that he was as quick as the next fella when it came to taking care of his own welfare, hadn't thought about their being on an island. They were practically trapped, if you looked at it that way. They were strangers in town, with no place to hide, and they were the kind who stuck out from the crowd, too. A man with a patch on his right eye, a big black, and a man with a deep Mississippi accent.

"There's nothing to worry about," he said, more to convince himself than the others. "The Colonel's got us out of many a tight spot in times past, and there's no reason to think this one is any different. Has he ever let us down before?"

The others shook their heads, but he could still see the doubt in their eyes. The doubt reflected what he himself felt, but he was loyal.

"I expect he's got us a private boat already chartered," he said. "For all we know, it'll be waiting in the surf right by the Pavilion."

"Maybe so," Tollie said, but he clearly wasn't convinced.

Seth didn't say anything, but the look on his face told anyone who glanced at him what he thought.

"Dammit," Patch said, "we got to trust the Colonel. He's the only one we ever trusted before, and he never failed us. Remember that time in Kansas?"

They remembered. They'd robbed a bank in some little town, trying to be like the James boys or somebody, and Seth had gotten his horse shot right out from under him. The Colonel, already free of the town, had turned his horse and seen what happened. Ignoring the rifle and pistol bullets flying all around him, he had ridden back into town, reached down and grabbed Seth by the belt, and carried him right on out of there. They'd ridden double for two days until the posse got off their trail, and Seth knew that he owed his life, or at least his liberty, to the Colonel.

"He would've done the same for any of us," Patch said.

The others nodded in agreement, and they parted.

But to tell the truth, all of them were still a little worried. Even Patch.

Jack went back to his cousin's whorehouse.

Annie was glad to see him. "I still got a little bre'fuss lef'," she said. "Those girls didn't eat hearty today."

Jack thanked her, ate scrambled eggs and bacon, and asked her if there had been any trouble the night before.

"Not one bit. Why? You 'spectin' somethin' to happen aroun' here? That why you laid out all night?"

"I just thought someone might have come looking for me," Jack said. "A friend," he added when she gave him a hard look.

"Didn't no friends of yours come by here. You ain't had time to make no friends, and you sure made you'self some kind of enemy when you come in here smellin' like you been rollin' in the privy. That fella you chased the one you think mighta come in here?"

"I thought he might have come looking for me, yes," Jack said.

"Pay a social call on you, is that it? See if you want to go out dancin' or somethin'?"

"Not exactly."

"I 'spect not. I 'spect he want to whip up on you for followin' him in the midnight like that. Man owe you money?"

"You might say that."

"Well, you can forget it. He ain't been aroun' here, and you be better off if you just let him be."

Jack mopped out his plate with a piece of light bread. "You're probably right, Annie," he said, his mouth full. "You're probably right."

Strate had decided to pay a visit to Sally Radford and explain to her why he hadn't been by to see her father the night before.

He located her address, a wood frame house that had been recently painted white, with a neatly tended flower garden and a huge oleander bush in the front yard.

He walked up the oyster-shell walk, climbed the steps, and knocked on the door. He was surprised when Sally answered it herself. He had been expecting someone else— her mother, perhaps.

"Well," she said, just looking at him, not opening the door much wider than a crack.

"I wanted to tell you something," Strate said.

"You don't have to tell me anything," she said.

He could tell that she was mad at him. He didn't know exactly why, however. He hadn't said that he would be there to meet her father, after all. That had been her idea, not his.

On the other hand, maybe he had led her to believe that he would be there. He could have told her about his plan to follow Patch from the docks, a plan that hadn't worked as well as he might have hoped. If he had talked to her father and gotten his help, things might have been different.

"I'm sorry I didn't come by last night," he said. "It was a mistake not to. I thought I could do something on my own."

He didn't know why he was explaining to her. He never had had to explain himself to anyone before, nor had he wanted to. He wondered why he was doing it now.

The door opened a little wider, or maybe it was just his imagination.

"What did you do?" Sally asked.

"I followed Patch home from the docks."

The door was definitely opening wider now.

"Did you catch up with him?" Sally asked.

"You might say that."

The door opened all the way.

"Well, come in and tell me all about it," Sally said. She was dressed in a plain cotton dress, this one with a high neck and lacy collar. Her hair was up in some kind of roll.

Strate thought she looked just as good this way as she had when her hair was down. Her eyes were browner than he had remembered, but maybe it was just the difference in the light.

"Is there, uh, anyone else here?" he said as he stepped inside.

"Were you expecting someone?"

"I thought that your mother might be here," Strate said.

When it came right down to it, he had to admit to himself that he had never called on a respectable woman at her home before. The women he had known in the last few years had lived mostly in hotels or in rooms above saloons, not in their own homes. He realized suddenly that he was basically a very conventional fellow, and that he really expected there would be someone in the house to chaperon them.

"My mother died ten years ago," Sally said, leading him to the parlor.

"Oh," he said. "I'm sorry."

"Are you uncomfortable being here alone with me?" She smiled at him. "Are you worried about what the neighbors might think about us?"

"Uh, no," he said. He was, but he would never admit it.

"Good," she said. "I stopped worrying about them years ago. They all think that since my mother died, *they* ought to be my mothers. Well, they aren't."

They entered the parlor. It was a bright room, with sunlight coming in through gauzy curtains. It was furnished with a love seat, three straight-backed chairs with plump cushion seats, several small tables, one of which supported a glass lamp, and a small bookshelf. Strate saw a Bible and a copy of *The Pilgrim's Progress* among the volumes on the shelves.

Sally sat in one of the chairs and indicated that Strate should take one of the others. When he was seated, she said, "Now tell me about what happened yesterday."

Strate gave her a short version of the events of the previous evening, making things sound much less dangerous than they had been.

"And you didn't get your money back."

"Not a penny of it."

"What will you do now? Follow him again?"

Strate told her that he didn't think Patch would be going back to the docks. "They have something planned for tonight, though," he added.

"How do you know that?"

He told her what he had overheard, and the conclusions he had drawn. "I sort of thought that maybe you and I could go to the ball," he said. He didn't understand why he was talking like that. He was usually straightforward in his speech. "Then if we saw them in the crowd, we could put a stop to whatever it is that they're up to."

"What do you think they might be up to?" She leaned forward slightly in the chair, and Strate found his eyes drawn to the line of her bosom. He didn't know what was the matter with him.

"I don't know what they might be planning. You think there's any chance they could rob the place?"

She shook her head, and a tendril of hair came loose from the roll. "I don't see how. There's no way someone could rob as many people as will be at the Pavilion to see Grant. Not even three people could do that."

Strate knew that she was right. It would take an army to rob that many people. He wondered if Patch's plans had anything to do with Grant. He couldn't imagine what, but it was true that Colonel Benson and his men had met during the war and that Benson had never really admitted that the war was over, having carried on his own little war for some time after Appomattox, according to what that man in Houston—Barney—had told him. Maybe Benson had some crazy idea about—Strate couldn't even think of anything.

Sally interrupted his thoughts. "You really must want that money back."

"It's a lot of money," he told her. "You said that yourself."

"I know it is, but still. . . ."

"There's more to it than just the money. They robbed me, is what they did. Shot me, kicked me, and left me lying in the dirt. I don't want them to get away with that." He didn't mention that in addition he had been bound, gagged, and almost thrown in Galveston Bay.

"If we did go to the Pavilion tonight, and if we did see them there, they might not be so happy with you."

"I hope that I see them first."

"You saw Patch first last night," she pointed out.

"This time will be different," he promised. "Jack is going to watch outside, and I'll be watching inside. We won't let them catch us together again."

"Jack is the Negro?"

"That's right."

"You said that he was helping you get it back, but you didn't say why."

Strate explained that Jack had some very good reasons for helping. "He didn't want to at first. I had to persuade him."

"Well," Sally said, "I'll help you, too. And you won't even have to give me any of your money."

"What will I have to give you?"

She smiled again. "Wait and see," she said.

Chapter Eighteen

Benson was cleaning his gun. It was a Model 1875 Remington .45 with nickeled steel, which looked much like the Colt Peacemaker. Benson, however, had always preferred the Remington, though he couldn't really have given a reason.

The gun's cylinder was lying on the polished wooden top of the table in Benson's new room, a much neater and nicer room than the one he had vacated. He had registered in this hotel under his own name and made no secret of the fact that he was in town to attend the ball at the Pavilion and that he hoped to get a glimpse of Grant while he was there. He had mentioned these facts to the desk clerk and to the young man who had carried his bags to the room.

He didn't recall exactly where he had picked up the Remington. Not in Kansas. That had been too long ago, and the Remington had come into his possession only a few years before. It was a good gun, with good balance, and it was certainly accurate. He had not fired it often, having had no occasion, really, in the last few years, but he had taken care to fire it enough to know exactly how it handled.

He reassembled the pistol carefully, a job made a bit awkward by the wooden hand, and loaded the chambers, leaving the one under the hammer empty. Then he slipped the gun into its holster, which was also lying on the table. It was made of smooth saddle leather, and it was also fairly new. Benson liked for his equipment to look good.

He planned to use the pistol that night, in a gesture that would make him a hero and a popular figure in the press.

He was going to kill the assassins of Grant and Cuney.

He hadn't told Patch that part of his plan, of course. He hadn't told anyone.

He thought it was a very neat plan.

Cuney would be dead.

Grant would probably be dead as well.

There would be many accusations tossed back and forth about who had set up the murders and who would profit from them the most.

There would be a dead black man and a dead white man at the scene, both of whom were dockworkers. The labor organizations would be suspected, especially if the word was spread about the real purpose of the meeting between Grant and Cuney.

Benson intended to spread the word, of course.

There would already be a great deal of unrest among the labor groups, much of it created by the two dead men, and Seth's rumors would be percolating through the city.

Seth would have to be dealt with, too, but Benson did not regard that as a problem. Seth would be quite easy to dispose of.

Tollie and Patch were a different matter, and he almost regretted what he was going to do to them. They were perfect for the job, however, and he had to use them.

He could see the newspaper stories now, the interviews. He would say that he had learned of what his two former associates intended to do, though they had not told him who their backers were. He would say that he tried to stop them but that he had arrived too late. Only then had he drawn his own weapon and killed them in self-defense.

It was a perfect plan. He could see no flaws in it. Patch would have appreciated it, if only Benson had been able to tell him.

If there was a flaw, that was it.

There was no one that he could tell how clever he had been.

Seth knew that the Colonel had told Patch he would meet them that night at nine, but the Colonel had also told Seth to meet him every day at his hotel at four o'clock. Seth had reported faithfully each day to tell the Colonel where he had been and what he had told the people he had talked to, or at least as much of it as he could remember. Seth knew that remembering was not his strong point.

So despite the fact that the Colonel would be meeting with all of them later, he went to the hotel at four, as usual.

The Colonel had told Seth to be careful about the hotel and not to let anyone see him visiting the room. That was an easy order to obey, since there never seemed to be anyone in the lobby except the desk clerk, who was never watching anything. Seth would slink through the lobby and be down the hall in nothing flat, tapping at the Colonel's door.

He didn't know why the Colonel chose to stay in such a ratty place, and he didn't ask. It was none of his business what the Colonel did.

His tapping was answered immediately. The door swung open suddenly, and there was the Colonel, dressed as he had always been since coming to Galveston, more like the old days than what Seth had seen him in more recently.

"Come in, Seth," the Colonel said, holding the door wide.

Seth stepped in, and the door shut behind him.

"Tell me, Seth, how did things go today?"

The Colonel began pacing around the tiny room, and it seemed to Seth that there was a touch of nervousness in his voice. Well, no wonder. It wasn't every day you killed a former president, or had him killed.

"Things went fine, Colonel," Seth said. "I talked to some insurance men down on the Strand, and to some other people, too. I don't know what the other people did for a living, though."

"That's all right, Seth. And what did you tell them?"

"What you said, Colonel. About the niggers taking over when the white men went on strike, and how Grant was behind it all."

"Fine, Seth, fine."

Seth wondered why the Colonel didn't stop pacing and sit down. For that matter, they both usually sat down when they had these little talks. He began to wonder if something funny was going on.

"Is something the matter, Colonel?" he said.

"No, no, nothing's the matter." Benson walked over to the window. "Come here, Seth. I want to show you something."

Curious, Seth walked over to the window. "What?" he said.

"Look," Benson said. "There."

He pointed out the window.

Seth looked, but he didn't see anything. Just the alley, which wasn't paved, and the wall of another building.

"There's nothing out there," he said.

"Oh, but there is," Benson said. "Bend over a little and look."

Seth bent over and peered through the glass. "I still don't—"

His words were cut short as Benson's wooden hand smashed into the back of his skull, making a sound like that of an oak plank hitting a melon.

Seth fell forward, his face hitting the floor in front of the window, though he didn't feel it. He would never feel anything again, which in a way was lucky for him.

The Colonel looked at Seth for a moment with an expression resembling regret on his face. Then he pulled the spread off the bed, placed it on the floor, and rolled Seth in it.

Seth was still breathing, though very faintly. Benson walked to the bed and pulled the lumpy feather pillow off. He carried the pillow over to Seth, knelt down, and mashed the pillow into Seth's face.

There was no struggle at all. Seth was too far gone to

struggle. Right before he died, he arched his back slightly. Then his heels kicked against the floor, their sound deadened by the spread.

They didn't kick long.

The Colonel walked to the window and opened it. He looked out to see if there was anyone in the alley. He had checked it several times in the past few days, but he had never seen anyone.

There was nobody now, either.

He had thought he might wrap Seth in the spread, but he now considered the fact that even a cheap hotel like this one would be likely to miss a spread, perhaps even more likely than a better establishment.

So there would be no covering for Seth.

He grasped the body under the armpits and hoisted it up. He dragged it the few inches to the window, shoved the head and shoulders out. Then he walked around to the feet, picked them up, and pushed Seth into the alley.

He followed his dead companion out the window. There was a trash heap only a few feet away, and as far as Benson had been able to tell, nothing had been taken from it in days. It had been added to, however. He thought that Seth would be safe in there, at least safe from discovery.

He wouldn't be safe from the rats, however. Benson had seen several rats around the pile of trash, rats as big as terriers. Well, Seth wouldn't mind, not now.

He cleared out a hollow at the rear of the pile, where the boxes could rest against the wall and not cause the whole thing to collapse. When he had cleared out a space that was large enough, he pushed Seth in.

Someone would probably smell him in a few days, though Benson wasn't sure that was absolutely to be expected. The pile already stank of rotten oranges and other unidentifiable things, and the alley reeked of the odors of the privy. Seth might not be discovered for weeks.

It didn't really matter. Whenever Seth was found would be too late to interfere with Benson's plans.

He concealed the body with the boxes he had taken from

the pile and strolled out of the alley as if he had no worries in the world.

And he didn't. Things were going along very well, just the way he had planned them.

Things were not going well for Phil Sheridan. While his room at the Tremont Hotel was comfortable and well furnished, he was extremely bothered by the mosquitoes. They were out in force, though it was only afternoon, because the generally reliable Gulf breeze had dropped to a low sigh. The pesky insects, never shy, were at their best when there was no wind to cause them trouble. They swarmed around Sheridan's face, humming their high-pitched hums as he brushed at them with his hands.

Sheridan left his room and went looking for Grant, who was not in. Grant had said earlier that he was going up to the hotel's lookout tower to see the sights, and Sheridan located the stairs.

Grant was indeed in the tower, gazing out over the docks and the calm waters of the bay. The mosquitoes did not seem to be troubling him at all.

"A beautiful sight," Grant said when he saw Sheridan, and it was true. The ships floated on the peaceful waters, their spars shining in the sunlight. The men bustling back and forth with the cotton bales seemed almost like silent automatons from the tower, and the seabirds wheeling through the air called loudly as they flew.

Sheridan forgot his complaint for a few minutes as he looked. They turned to the Gulf side and watched the low waves creep up on the shore. They could almost, but not quite, hear them. It was more as if they could feel them, as if the old rhythm of the sea were a part of the rhythm of their hearts and bodies.

There were no mosquitoes in the tower, Sheridan noticed. It might have been that the slight breeze was just the tiniest bit stronger here, or it might have been that the mosquitoes didn't like to fly that high, Sheridan didn't care, as long as they weren't bothering him.

He rubbed at his neck ruefully where several small bumps were forming, souvenirs of the attacks in his room.

"The dinner here tonight should be quite good," Grant said. "This place has a wonderful reputation for food."

"I hope that the blasted mosquitoes are gone by then," Sheridan said. "I'm not sure that I can eat with them sinking their snouts in me."

Grant laughed. "Then you haven't changed your opinion about which place you would live in and which one you would rent out?"

"Not in the least," Sheridan said. "Are you sure that I must go to the ball with you later on?"

"I don't think it will be necessary. I won't really be going to the ball, you see. I will be meeting with Cuney in another part of the building. I will merely put in an appearance at the ball, then go to the meeting."

"I may stay here, then," Sheridan said. "With all my windows closed. I may suffocate, but at least the plaguey bugs will be shut outside."

"That would be fine," Grant said. "I believe the president has overstated the danger of this trip. There has been absolutely no threat so far."

"Good," Sheridan said, still rubbing his neck. "I wonder if a stiff drink of whiskey would discourage the things."

"Probably not," Grant said, "but it might make the stinging less tiresome."

"I agree. It is certainly worth a try."

They descended the steps to the bar to find out.

Norris Cuney was staying in a private home. He was not bothered by the mosquitoes, or at least he was not bothered by them as much as Phil Sheridan was.

Cuney had other things on his mind, such as the success of his meeting with President Grant. Cuney very much wanted the meeting to go well, not because of any worries about his personal goals but because of his goals for the black men of Texas.

He sat in his room looking out, not at the Gulf or the docks but at a large oak tree that grew in the yard of the house where he was staying. The tree was clearly very old, its thick, gnarled trunk and limbs shaped by the prevailing winds of the island.

Black folks were like that tree, he thought. Shoved this way and that by the winds of chance and circumstance, being shaped by the winds but not conquered by them, and enduring to at last become something solid and permanent.

The tree was thickly hung with Spanish moss, grayish-green and dangling, and the moss would one day kill it. Cuney wondered where the moss would fit into his little allegory, then decided that it would be best to ignore it. Nothing was going to kill his race, and tonight's talk would put forward their cause.

The thought of a strike by the white workers did not appeal to Cuney; he could see the possibility for damage if things divided along racial lines, as they were sure to do. All he wanted was for the black workers to receive equal wages with the whites, while the whites wanted even higher wages than they were already receiving.

Cuney had heard from some of his friends in town the rumors that were making the rounds of the docks, but they were clearly ridiculous. No one in his right mind would believe them. Or so it would seem. One could never tell about things like that, especially if things were presented in the right light. He admitted to himself that the possibility for violence did indeed exist, as unlikely as he thought it.

Of one thing he was absolutely convinced, however. The dockowners could not afford to have the white workers walk out of their jobs. At present, though the blacks did have a number of men there, a white walkout would virtually paralyze the shipping industry, and that paralysis would mean the death of Galveston.

He thought about that for a while. Suppose there really were a strike by the whites. Suppose he offered to organize all the blacks in the area and get the industry going again.

He dismissed the thought. In the current situation it was impossible to consider it. There would be an outbreak of bloodshed for sure, and that was something to be avoided. He would lobby for equal wages, for equal treatment, and hope to get something close to that. Anything else would be too much to hope for.

He wondered what kind of man Grant was, and how it would be to talk to him.

All in all, it looked to be a very interesting evening.

Chapter Nineteen

By late that afternoon, Lee Strate knew that he had found what he had been looking for when he left Kansas. He hadn't known it at the time, but he had been looking for Sally Radford. He had looked in a lot of strange places, in a lot of strange ways, and for a while he had even been in possession of five thousand dollars as a result of his looking.

In a way, he thought, he even owed Patch a favor. If he hadn't been led to Galveston, he never would have found what he was looking for.

Not that he felt any more favorably disposed toward Patch. Not in the least. But he certainly felt happy for himself.

He had spent the day at Sally's house, and she had even fixed his lunch. They had spent a great deal of time talking about the things they had done, the things they liked, and the things they didn't like. Strate was amazed by how much they had in common.

Sally confessed that she had stayed in Galveston only because of her father.

"I take care of him," she said. "He doesn't really need me, but it does him good to think he does. And he likes to think I need him, too. My mother's death was harder on him than it was on me, I think. He didn't know what to do with a daughter, and he didn't think he could bring me up all by himself. So we made a sort of pact. We said we'd help each other, and that's what we did. We've gotten past the stage where we need each other's help now, but I'm not sure he wants to admit that.''

"And the neighbors must have thought that the two of you needed a good woman in the house,'' Strate guessed.

"That's right.'' They were back in the parlor now; the sun had moved away from the window and the light in the room was subdued. Sally's face was in shadow. "They didn't think a big, rough man could do the things a girl needed done, and they all set out to see that the right woman got moved in. But my father isn't the kind to be pushed into anything, much less something like marriage. He's stubborn that way.''

"Not that it runs in the family,'' Strate said, but he was smiling.

Sally tilted her head and looked at him, but she was smiling, too. "Of course it does,'' she said. "And maybe I've been a little too eager to show them that they can't tell us Radfords how to behave or what to do, but I can't see that it's hurt them any.'' She thought about it for a minute. "Or changed them any.''

"And they haven't had much luck at changing you,'' Strate observed.

"They never will,'' she said. "And neither will you.''

"Who said I was going to try?''

"I just didn't want you getting any ideas.'' She moved her chair closer to his. "I can tell that we're going to be seeing a lot of each other, and I want you to know how I am about things.''

"I know, all right, but don't worry. I like you just the way you are.''

"And you feel the same way I do, about us seeing each other?''

"Yes,'' Strate said. "I surely do.''

By the time her father got home, Sally and Strate knew each other better than many couples who had spent years together.

Sally made the introductions.

Radford looked all in, as if he had spent a tiring day on the docks, which he had, but he stuck out his hand.

Strate took it and shook. "Glad to meet you, sir," he said.

"You known my daughter long?" Radford said suspiciously.

Strate explained how he and Sally had met at the greased-pig scramble.

"Huh," Radford said. "I knew she ought to keep away from those things."

"Mr. Strate is a very nice young man," Sally said. "He's here on business, and don't look at him that way. He's not the first man I've invited here. Besides, he wants to talk to you about someone."

"Let's go inside, then, where a man can get a drink of water."

They went into the kitchen and sat at the square wooden table. Radford drank two tall glasses of water.

"Rustlin' that cotton is a thirsty business," he said, setting the glass down on the tabletop. "Now what's this about you askin' me about someone?"

"I came here looking for a man," Strate said. Then he described Patch. "Your daughter said you knew him."

"Wouldn't say that. I'm acquainted with him."

"He stole some money from me," Strate said. "That's why I'm here."

"Can't say that I'm surprised. He seems like the type."

"What I can't figure out is why he's working at the docks when he has all my money," Strate said.

"Well, now, I might can help you with that. He's there to make trouble, the way I see it."

Sally poured her father another glass of water from a glazed pitcher with roses painted on it. He took a long drink.

"What kind of trouble?" Strate asked.

Radford wiped his mouth with the back of his hand. "Between the Cotton Jammers and the Screwmen." He told Strate a little about Patch's line of talk on the job.

"Somebody got him that job, probably paid him to stir things up. I wondered what he was doing there, myself."

"Has he been successful at it?" Strate asked. "At making trouble, I mean?"

"I'd say so. Have to admit he even got me a little bit riled, the way he was goin' on, and some of the other fellas are even more upset about it than I am."

Strate had no idea why Patch would be making trouble, but he did wonder if Tollie was doing the same thing on his own job. Well, it didn't matter. The important thing was to get his money back, not to keep them from making a living on the docks and stirring up trouble there.

"Can you tell me anything else about him?" Strate asked.

"Not a thing. Don't like the fella much, that's all."

Strate dismissed the docks from his mind. "I'd like to take Sally to the ball at the Pavilion tonight," he said. "If it's all right with you."

Radford laughed, a big booming sound filling up the kitchen. "Son, she's been doing whatever she wants to for years around here. If she wants to go to that ball, what I say don't matter a thing."

"I don't have anything to wear, though," Strate said. Even if he went back to his own room, there wouldn't be a suit there.

"I used to wear a suit, years ago," Radford said. "We're about the same size. If the moths haven't eaten it and it'll fit you, you're welcome to it. Sally can show you where it is, in that big closet we don't use anymore. Me, I just want to get cleaned up and go to bed."

They left him at the table, and Sally took Strate to a musty room behind a closed door.

"This was their room," she said. "He doesn't come in here."

The suit was in the closet, a little mildewed but not entirely unpresentable. Sally was sure that she could get it cleaned up in time for the festivities.

While she worked on it, Strate went out and bought a fish at the market. Sally fried it for supper.

*   *   *

They caught the trolley to the Pavilion. Sally paid. She was dressed in a long black gown with a high neck and looked more respectable than any one of her neighbors would have believed. Strate thought she was beautiful.

It was after dark, and the Pavilion was already jammed, the crowds flowing this way and that, those in the middle of the floor dancing to the music of the band, a larger and louder group than had been there on Strate's first trip.

Strate overheard several people talking about having seen Grant.

"Looks just like the picture," one man commented.

"But shorter," his female companion said.

"Well," the man said, "it's hard to judge a man's height by his picture."

"Perhaps, but it *was* disappointing."

They drifted off into the crowd.

"What we have to do," Strate told Sally, "is make our way through this mob and see if we can find Patch." Even as he said it, he almost gave up hope. There were just too many people. Even a man who stood out like Patch was going to be almost impossible to spot.

Nevertheless they had to try.

Strate soon realized that the job was even trickier than he had thought. He had believed the Pavilion to be crowded during the greased-pig scramble, but that group had been only a fraction the size of this one.

He felt hot and awkward in the unfamiliar suit as he pushed through the people, trying to spot a familiar face. He kept Sally's arm in his as they tried to skirt around the edges of the crowd, and it was virtually impossible to say anything to her because of the babbling all around them, which mixed with the playing of the band and echoed off the high ceiling and the walls.

It took them half an hour to make a circuit of the floor. In that time they had been shoved, jostled, elbowed, and stepped on enough to last them a lifetime. And they still had not spotted Patch or any of the others.

"I guess I could have been wrong," Strate said, his mouth near Sally's ear. "I was sure they'd be here, though."

They were near the beach entrance, and Sally did not try to answer him. Instead she tugged on his hand and he followed her outside.

It was a relief to get out. Though the air was heavy and muggy, it was not as oppressive as that inside the building. Crowded as the place was with dancers and spectators, it was almost impossible to get a deep breath.

Strate looked up at the sky. The breeze had picked up a bit, and the clouds had increased. They moved slowly across the face of the moon. Behind him, the Pavilion blazed with the light of its many lanterns and gaslights. He realized that he had not yet seen the electric light that gave the place its name.

When they had breathed in some of the night air, Sally said, "Maybe they were going to meet outside."

There were many others outside on the porch and walking on the beach. Many of the men had come out to smoke cigars, and the couples had come for at least a minimum of privacy.

"Jack's supposed to be out here somewhere," Strate told her. "He thought they might get together out here and then go in."

Sally looked around them. "I don't see him," she said.

Strate didn't see him, either. "Let's go down on the beach," he said.

They walked down the wooden steps and stood for a minute, both of them looking to the right and left for some sign of Jack. It was darker down there, away from the building, and they didn't see the man running toward them until he was almost on them.

It was Jack.

"I saw them," he said, not waiting to be introduced to Sally. "They're around at that end by the tower."

"Sally, this is Jack," Strate said. "He's the friend I told you about."

"Pleased to meet you," Sally said.

"Likewise," Jack said. "I'm sorry that the circumstances aren't better, but we need to hurry. They may be gone by the time we get back there."

"You stay here," Strate told Sally. Jack had already turned and started away, and Strate went after him.

Sally was right behind him. "I'm not staying anywhere," she said to Strate's back.

He did not try to stop her or argue with her. He was afraid of losing sight of Jack.

The tower was on the east end of the building and was actually no taller than the Pavilion itself, about three stories. It was called a tower only because of its shape.

When they arrived, there was no one near it. All the people at the ball were either inside the Pavilion or on the porch, and though the buildings were connected, there was no reason for anyone at the Pavilion to enter the tower. It was used mainly for sleeping quarters for musicians, meetings of small groups, and the like.

"They were right here a minute ago," Jack said. "I guess I should have stayed with them, but I wanted to locate you if I could. I didn't feel like talking to them while I was by myself."

"I don't plan to talk to them at all, not unless I've got a gun in my hand," Strate said. He pushed back his coat to show Jack the pistol that was holstered at his side. "Where do you think they went?"

"There's only one place they could go," Sally said. "You can see that they didn't pass by us, and there's no one walking down by the water here. So they must be inside."

"We'll go in and have a look," Strate said. "I wish you'd stay here, though," he went on, addressing Sally. He remembered the last time he'd entered a building while following Patch. He didn't think he would be caught off-guard again, but if he was, he didn't want Sally involved.

Then he had an inspiration. "If we aren't out in fifteen minutes, you can raise a ruckus. Or get the police. That would be even better."

Sally didn't seem too pleased with the idea, but she saw the sense of it. "All right," she said. "But you better come back."

"Don't worry, we will." Strate turned to Jack. "How many of them were there?"

"Three," Jack said. "But one of them was different. It must have been the Colonel."

"Which one was missing?"

"The white man who took us to the docks."

Strate wondered if Mush-mouth was lurking somewhere nearby, waiting to see if anyone followed his friends. There was no need to worry about it, however. If he was there, he was there.

And if he was there, he might try something with Sally.

"Do you have a gun?" Strate said.

"Not me," Jack said. "I might shoot myself. I've got this, though." He showed Strate the knife he had taken from the dead seaman.

Strate had thought he might leave a pistol with Sally, but the knife would not be much help to her. She was not an ordinary woman, but he was virtually certain she knew nothing about knife fighting.

They would just have to take the chance that there was no one watching. Better yet, he could send her farther away.

"I think you might be safer if you went back to the Pavilion, Sally," he said. "That way, if there's anyone watching out here, he can't get to you. Give us fifteen minutes before you sound any alarms."

"I'll wait here," she said.

Strate had not known her for long, but he had known her long enough to know that argument would do no good.

"All right," he said. "Don't wander off."

"I won't."

Strate drew his pistol. He liked the way it felt in his hand. "Where's the door?" he asked.

"I think there's one around on the other side," Jack said.

"Let's go, then."

They left Sally and walked around to the side of the tower. There was a door, all right, and it was open onto an entrance room that would have seemed fairly large had not Strate just come from the Pavilion.

There didn't seem to be anyone in the room, but Strate and Jack mounted the steps as silently as they could.

The light flickered and cast shadows on the walls. There was no one there.

Across the room to their right was a stairway. On the left were French doors opening into another room, but that room was dark.

"The stairs?" Strate asked.

"May as well give them a try," Jack said.

The stairs were dark. Strate had the Peacemaker, so he took the lead as they began to climb.

Chapter Twenty

In a room on the third floor of the tower, Norris Cuney and Ulysses S. Grant faced each other across a small wooden table. There was a sideboard in the room, and on it were a bottle of whiskey, a small pitcher of ice water, and several glasses. Both men had drinks in front of them.

To one side of the table was a coal-oil lamp. It put out only a small amount of heat, but in the already warm room it made things significantly warmer.

Grant wiped his brow with a large white kerchief and took a swallow of his drink. "What do you mean by saying that you believe there will be no violence?" he asked Cuney.

The black man smiled. He was wearing a dark suit, but he seemed not to feel the heat in the room. His brow appeared cool, and the light glowed in his chocolate eyes.

"The dockowners will not permit it," he said. "They cannot afford a work stoppage of any kind, and if one occurs, I will bring in my black men to do the jobs. We ask only a fair wage—the same wage that the white workers are being paid. For that we will keep the docks going and risk the violence. But I repeat, there will be none."

"I wish I could be that sure," Grant said.

"You can be," Cuney said. He sipped delicately at his drink, which was watered considerably more than Grant's. "The rumors that are circulating are nothing more than that—rumors. The white men will see that there is nothing to be gained from fighting. After a few days, or a few weeks at most, they will return to their jobs, or to the jobs that remain. Most of them will find work again, and any bitterness will be forgotten."

Grant shook his head. He still was not convinced, but he was hoping that Cuney was accurate in his analysis. If he was, then President Hayes would be well pleased with the results of Grant's trip. True, Grant still had to meet with the governor, but if he could report that all was well, the governor would be even more pleased than Hayes, or so Grant surmised.

"What will be the result of all this for you?" Grant asked.

Cuney shook his head and tried to look modest. "I hope for nothing for myself," he said. "Of course, if the president or the governor were to see fit to appoint me to some small position, I would have no objections."

Maybe it would really be that easy, Grant thought. Maybe his trip had really been nothing more than a pleasure jaunt, with Hayes merely imagining all the possible trouble that could break loose in Texas. Galveston certainly seemed peaceful enough, he had to admit.

At that moment he heard a noise in the hall. He looked up to see two men in the doorway, a black man and a white one.

Both of them were holding revolvers.

Colonel Benson was holding a revolver, too. He was standing a few paces behind Patch and Tollie, ready to kill them both, though not until after they had done what he sent them there to do. They would be the villains, and he would be the hero. He had one more momentary twinge of regret at what he was about to do, had one last thought of the two men and their loyalty, of the times they had spent together.

Then he dismissed all such considerations from his mind.

"Now," he said.

Strate reached the top of the stairs at that instant. "Just hold on," he said. He didn't know what was going on, but he didn't like the sight that greeted him in the dim hallway: a man with a gun, Patch and Tollie silhouetted in the doorway, also with drawn pistols.

Benson did not know who the intruders were, but he thought they might be excellent witnesses to his heroism, if Patch and Tollie would just do their part.

Unfortunately those two had turned to see what was going on in the hallway.

"Dammit!" Benson yelled. "Do your work."

In the room, Grant was already scrambling for cover, though there was little to be had. With a soldier's instinct he headed for the sideboard.

Patch turned back and got off a shot, shattering the whiskey bottle and sending shards of glass flying. One small piece cut Grant's cheek as he hit the floor and skidded to the wall by the sideboard.

Tollie fired at Cuney, but the black man kicked over the table and dived backward. The bullet missed him by a foot.

The lamp hit the floor, and the fuel reservoir broke. Coal oil spread across the wooden floor, carrying flame with it.

"They're trying to kill the president!" Benson yelled, firing in the direction of Patch and Tollie.

The fire touched window curtains and raced up the wall.

Strate had no idea what was going on.

Jack had come into the hall behind him and was staring at the doorway. He had no more idea than Strate about the meaning of all the confusion, but he could see that there was a fire. Already the doorway looked like the gate of hell.

Patch and Tollie never dreamed that Benson was firing at them. They turned and got off quick shots at Strate and Jack, standing with their backs to the doorway.

The fire was spreading rapidly. The room was practically

an inferno, and it dawned on Strate that Grant might very well be in there. He shot Benson, who tumbled back into the room, falling between Patch and Tollie.

Neither man turned to help him. They fired their guns at Strate instead.

"You son of a bitch!" Patch screamed. "This time you're done for!"

Bullets slapped into the wall near Strate. He was about to return their fire when two figures smashed into their backs, knocking them sprawling.

Grant and Cuney stumbled over the prone men, gagging and coughing from the smoke that had filled the room and was now beginning to pour into the hall.

"This whole place is going up any minute," Jack said.

"You help those two get down the stairs," Strate told him. "I'm going to get my goddamn money."

"All right," Jack said. "But I wouldn't linger up here if I were you."

Grant and Cuney didn't wait for his help. They began to make their way down the stairs, but they could hardly see where they were going because of their well-smoked eyes. Jack stepped down beside them and took their elbows.

"This way, gentlemen," he said.

Tollie and Patch were getting up. They had been flattened, but they hadn't lost hold of their pistols.

Patch got to his knees and fired, shooting off the heel of Strate's left boot.

Strate lost his balance and fell to the floor, firing as he fell.

Tollie was hit and pitched backward into the wall. His pistol fired into the ceiling.

Patch didn't waste a shot. He was standing now, and he stepped quickly over to Strate and kicked him in the head.

Strate's teeth slapped together and his mind went black. He didn't even hear his head hit the wooden floor.

*   *   *

Strate didn't know how long he was out, but it couldn't have been long. The fire had not spread much farther, but he could feel the heat of it licking out of the room.

Tollie still sat propped against the opposite wall. Strate could see now that Tollie wouldn't be going anywhere, and that the fire wouldn't bother him in the least. There was a red stain on the front of Tollie's shirt, just about over his heart.

"Lucky shot," Strate said aloud to no one in particular.

Through the doorway he could see the Colonel lying on his back. The flames had reached his wooden hand at the end of his outstretched arm. The hand was on fire.

Strate didn't know how long he had, but he thought it might be only seconds. Still, he was going to look. He inched over to Tollie's body and searched the dead man's pockets.

Sure enough, the money was there, or at least some of it was. It was just about how you would figure it. Men like Patch and Tollie didn't trust anyone but themselves. The safest place to keep money was on your person.

The money was in a tight roll. Strate didn't take time to count it. He stood up and began to walk to the stairs.

He heard something behind him and turned.

It was Benson. He no longer held his pistol, and his hand was aflame. He swung it in a roundhouse swing at Strate's jaw.

Strate got his arm up in time to block the blow partially, but it staggered him. He stumbled to the wall, and Benson went right by him, headed for the stairs.

There was a strange movement, as if the building had suddenly shifted, and then the roof of the room caved in. It made a muffled crash, sending sparks flying through the doorway and all along the hall. One of the walls suddenly burst into flame.

Strate followed Benson to the stairs.

By the time they got to the beach, the Pavilion had begun to empty. There were people running and screaming everywhere. Flames were shooting out of the top of the tower, which looked like some kind of Fourth of July rocket, and as Strate watched, the part that looked like a belfry toppled slowly over and landed on the roof of the Pavilion. It did not break through, but the roof immediately broke into flames.

Strate looked for Jack and Sally, but he could see neither of them in the milling throng. Everyone was yelling something different, but he thought most of them were calling for the fire department. Several times he was nearly knocked down as he tried to keep his balance on the boot with no heel.

He finally spotted two figures running down the beach.

One of them had a burning hand.

He pulled off both boots, tossed them aside, and began to run.

Everything had gone wrong for Benson. He didn't know for sure that Grant had escaped the fire, but he knew that Tollie was dead and that Patch was escaping. Two men had seen what was happening, and there was little likelihood that he was ever going to be declared a hero. In fact, there seemed every possibility that he would be sought as part of the assassination attempt, and his alibi, that he was merely trying to stop it, would not hold up.

Not if Patch had anything to say about it.

So he was going to kill Patch.

He didn't know how, but he was going to do it. He simply had to catch him first.

The charred hand at his side had almost stopped burning now. He hardly felt the pain that it had caused him moments before. The hard oak was too solid to burn for long, but it would continue to smolder. He wanted to stop and take it off, or at least soak it in the Gulf, but he didn't have the time. He was gaining on Patch, and he didn't want to lose the ground.

Patch now represented to him all his frustrations. If he could just stop him, things would be all right. There would be no one to say what the plot had been, no one to contradict his own version of the story.

He caught up with Patch at the edge of the waterline, no more than five hundred yards from the Pavilion, and threw himself at the big man's back. They fell into the shallow surf, rolling over and over.

Patch came up spitting and struggling.

"What the hell, Colonel? What the—"

Benson hit him with the charred hand, which shattered when it connected. Sparks flew over the water like fireflies.

Patch fell backward into the surf.

The Colonel sat on his chest and began to choke him with his good hand, holding his head beneath the water.

Patch braced his heels on the firm sand and bucked like a bronc, throwing the Colonel aside and breaking his grip. He threw himself across the Colonel's chest and tried to hold him down.

"What the hell?" he sputtered, spitting water. "What the hell?"

The Colonel's hand shot out of the water, grabbing Patch's hair. With a grip like stone he dragged Patch's head down below the surface, at the same time bringing his own face out of the water.

The Colonel fought to sit up, meanwhile keeping his tight grip on Patch's hair. Patch was thrashing like a gaffed fish, but he could not break the grip.

The water was not deep, but it was deep enough. By the time Strate got there, Patch was through struggling. The small waves rocked him gently as they broke on the shore, his boots touching the sand and hardly in the water at all.

"He tried to kill the president," Benson said. "I stopped him."

Strate looked at the body in the water. "I'd say you did that, all right." He drew his pistol and leveled it at Benson. "You just sit where you are for a minute."

He didn't really want to do it, but he was going to look through Patch's pockets. He had to holster the gun to do it.

Patch's pants were soaked and tight, but Strate got his hand in the pockets. The roll of money was in the right front. He pulled it out and put it in his own pocket, along with the roll he had taken from Tollie. He didn't feel any satisfaction that they were dead. In fact, he hardly felt any satisfaction that he had his money back. It didn't seem to mean a thing to him.

He pulled Benson to his feet.

"Let's go tell the president what a hero you are," he said.

The Pavilion was practically gone when they got back. Its red glow lit up the whole sky, but it would not do so for long. There would be nothing left. The structure had been entirely of wood, and it had burned so quickly that Strate was amazed. It could have been no more than thirty minutes since he had started up the stairs, if that long.

The crowd had calmed now, most of them standing silently watching the last of the burning. They were standing well back from the flames, and Strate could feel the heat even on the edges of the crowd.

He finally spotted Jack, along with a man who looked like President Grant and a well-dressed black man. Strate was suddenly conscious that he had ruined Radford's suit.

He led Benson over to where Jack and the others were standing.

"President Grant?" he asked.

Grant turned. "Yes?"

"I think this man has a story to tell you," Strate said.

Grant looked at the Colonel. Comprehension dawned in his eyes. "Benson," he said.

Patch was dead and could tell them nothing, but Grant was alive. Grant had always hated him, and now he would ruin everything. And beside him were two black men, the kind of men who had always spoiled things for Benson, always meant the destruction of everything that mattered.

Benson dived for them.

There was nothing Strate could do. Benson had been too quick for him.

But not too quick for Jack.

Benson came to a sudden stop at the end of Jack's right arm. He stumbled backward, and Strate could see the hilt of the sailor's knife sticking out of Benson's chest.

Benson looked down at the knife in amazement, as if he couldn't believe it was there, or that he was still alive.

He reached for the hilt with his good hand and tried to pull the knife out. He couldn't budge it.

He looked up at Cuney, then at Jack.

"Niggers," he said. Then he pitched forward in the sand.

Chapter Twenty-one

The next day Strate, Jack, and Sally sat on the Radford porch drinking lemonade.

"I 'spec' I'se de firs' black man to sit on white fokes po'ch in this whole town," Jack said.

"You're doing that again," Strate told him.

"Sorry," Jack said. "I couldn't resist. It's not every day I get to celebrate saving the life of a former president."

"You two are really something," Sally said. "I couldn't believe it when I found you standing there with Mr. Ulysses S. Grant."

"That's *General* Grant," Strate said. "Or President Grant."

"Don't go getting the big head," Sally said. "Even if you did save him."

It had taken a while to sort things out the previous night, but eventually Strate and Jack had been able to convince Grant and Cuney of what had happened. They had left out the part about the five thousand dollars, saying only that Patch and Tollie had tried to rob them and dump them in the harbor.

Grant explained that the two were "known associates" of Colonel Benson, who was a thorn in the side of the Union. "A constant troublemaker," Grant said, "and one I am sure was trying to kill me.'' He looked at Cuney. "Or both of us.''

"And no doubt the cause of all the rumors that were circulating,'' Cuney said. "Can you imagine the furor on the docks if either or both of us had died in there?''

They all stared at the glowing embers of what had once been the Electric Pavilion and its tower.

"I think we might be able to head off any trouble that was coming,'' Strate said.

"And how might that be?'' Grant asked.

Strate explained that Sally's father worked on the docks and that he could have some influence in squelching any rumors that Patch had spread. "Especially when he finds out that Patch was trying to kill you, General Grant. It's easy to see that Benson had his men out trying to stir up trouble for some reason or another.''

"I suppose that we'll never know exactly why,'' Grant said. "But a man with his record might have many reasons.''

Cuney had nothing more to say. He had actually hoped to come out of things better than he had, but he could wait. He was a patient man, and if the strike didn't come this year, as it now seemed it would not, it would come sooner or later. Things would be forgotten, as Cuney well knew. Even the attempted murder of a man like Grant would not be the topic of conversation forever.

In fact, it might not even get to be the topic in the first place. In all the confusion of the fire, no one had noticed anything else that was going on. If a couple of dead men were found on the beach, who was to say what they might have been doing there? There would be no reason to make a connection between them and the bones of another man that might or might not be found in the remains of the fire later on.

When Cuney expressed that thought to Grant, the general was in agreement with its intent. The group walked slowly away from Benson's body, leaving it where it lay in the sand. No one seemed to notice.

When they were some distance away, the reporters who

had come to the scene recognized Grant and Cuney and surrounded them. Strate, Jack, and Sally kept on walking. There was nothing to keep them there.

Jack finished off his glass of lemonade and sighed. "What do you think happened to the rest of the money?" he said.

It was something Strate had thought about for most of the night. He had recovered less than two thousand dollars.

"I guess they stashed some of it," he said. "And Mushmouth must have had his share, but who knows where he might be. He's just lucky that he wasn't around last night."

Seth had had his share, all right, but where he was, it would never do him any good. Already rats had gnawed him.

"It's still a lot of money," Jack said.

"I know that," Strate said.

"I don't have to take half of it," Jack said. "I could just take five hundred."

"A promise is a promise," Strate said. He looked out over the neighborhood, the peaceful houses and the oleander bushes. He looked at Sally. "Besides, I might be staying around here for a while. I might even get a job, earn my keep."

"All right," Jack said. "If that's what you want to do."

"You can buy William some oats," Strate said. "And I want to give you a little more money. Five hundred more."

Jack didn't understand, and Strate couldn't really explain. He had been trying to get that money back for so long that he really hadn't thought about what he would do when he got it. Now that he had it, it didn't seem to matter so much. In fact, compared to some other things, it didn't matter at all. The money had meant something to him once, but he couldn't remember what or why.

"It's for Aaron," Strate said. "He's having a hard time of it up there, and he can use it. I won't be needing it."

"You sure?"

"I think he might be able to get a job on the docks," Sally said. "If he wants one."

"That, or something," Strate said. "As long as I can stay here." He reached over and took Sally's hand.

"Well, I can't see any fault in that," Jack said. "Aaron will appreciate it a lot."

Strate handed him the money.

"Just tell him it came out of your share," Strate said. He thought about the shy children, hiding behind the skirts of their mother. "And say hello to William for me."

"I'll do that," Jack said. He stood up and put out his hand.

Strate took it, and they shook.

"I'm glad it was you that came by," Strate said.

"Me, too," Jack said. "Maybe I'll come for a visit sometime."

"You do that," Sally said. "You'd be welcome."

Jack walked down the porch steps and away down the street.

"You think he'll ever come back?" Sally asked.

"I don't know," Strate said. "I hope so."

The Gulf breeze ruffled Sally's hair. Strate wondered for a moment how far it was to Kansas, and if he'd ever go back.

Then he looked into Sally's eyes and knew it didn't matter.

Historical Note

This story is loosely based on actual historic events. Ulysses S. Grant did visit Galveston in 1880 in the company of Phil Sheridan, but there was no assassination attempt, or at least there is none on record.

The Electric Pavilion did in fact exist, but it was not completed until 1881. It burned in 1883.

The strike threatened in the novel finally took place in 1883, when the white longshoremen walked off the job. A Negro Longshoremen's Association was organized by Norris Cuney (the Cotton Jammers had been in existence since 1879), and the blacks took over all the work on the docks, being paid the same wages that the whites had been earning. There was no violence, and later Cuney became the port of Galveston's chief collector of customs.

About the Author

BILL CRIDER, mystery writer and professor of English at Alvin Community College, holds a Ph.D. from the University of Texas in Austin. He lives in Alvin, Texas with his wife and children. He is well-known to mystery readers as the winner of the 1986 Anthony Award for his mystery novel, TOO LATE TO DIE.

The
Old West
From

RICHARD S. WHEELER

100 ✓